Caroline unbuttoned the stranger's shirt....

"This is what I want you to do," she said haughtily. "When my mother comes, gaze at me like we're having these big romantic feelings or something. And then, just follow my lead. Now!" Caroline exclaimed, hearing footsteps. She tilted her head back. "Kiss me!"

Rick didn't play puppet on a string for anyone, but he'd come here with an ulterior motive concerning Caroline, so he didn't mind playing along. "Kiss you?" he drawled.

"Kiss me!"

"If duty calls..." he said and grinned wickedly. He bent her backward from the waist and lowered his mouth, not expecting her lips to taste quite so good or feel quite so soft. At their touch, everything about this crazy ploy stopped.

"Who are you?" Caroline's mother demanded, sweeping into the room.

"Rick Cassidy, ma'am," Caroline heard the stranger say. "And I'm very serious about your daughter."

ABOUT THE AUTHOR

Cathy Gillen Thacker is a full-time novelist who once taught piano to children. Born and raised in Ohio, she attended Miami University. After moving cross-country several times, she settled in Texas with her husband and three children. *Fiancé for Sale* is Cathy's thirty-third novel.

Books by Cathy Gillen Thacker

HARLEQUIN AMERICAN ROMANCE

HARLEQUIN INTRIGUE

Don't miss any of our special offers. Write to us at the following address for information on our newest releases.

Harlequin Reader Service
P.O. Box 1397, Buffalo, NY 14240
Canadian address: P.O. Box 603,
Fort Erie, Ont. L2A 5X3

Cathy Gillen Thacker

FIANCÉ FOR SALE

Harlequin Books

TORONTO • NEW YORK • LONDON
AMSTERDAM • PARIS • SYDNEY • HAMBURG
STOCKHOLM • ATHENS • TOKYO • MILAN
MADRID • WARSAW • BUDAPEST • AUCKLAND

Published July 1993

ISBN 0-373-16494-7

FIANCÉ FOR SALE

Chapter One

"I need your help."

This was going to be easier than he'd figured, Rick Cassidy thought as he set down the carton of glasses, shook the rainwater off his black Stetson and shrugged out of his soaked denim range coat. He shoved his fingers through his dark hair, doing his best to restore order to the damp tousled strands and met Caroline Lord's glance evenly.

He had known sneaking into the River Oaks estate, masquerading as a caterer, had been a risk. But he'd never expected to have the beautiful twenty-nine-year-old heiress dash down the back stairs and single him out.

"Yes, ma'am," he finally said deferentially, trying not to look too pleased with the unexpected turn of events. "I'll be glad to help you in any way I can."

"Good." Caroline Lord smiled at him briskly. "But you'll have to hurry." She tossed her dark curly hair and the skirt of her red silk taffeta ball gown swished alluringly. "We don't have much time." Grabbing his hand, she pulled him after her, in a mad dash up the stairs.

A wing of luxuriantly appointed bedrooms passed in a blur. He drank in the scent of her perfume. Or was it her? It was like nothing he had ever smelled. Like a whole field of wildflowers on a hot, sunny day. And her hand. God, it was soft and feminine, just right in his.

His fantasies were getting out of hand. He was here for business reasons, and business reasons only, Rick reminded himself sternly as she drew him into a pink-and-white bedroom strewn with expensive clothing he figured had to be hers.

"Listen, princess, I think you have the wrong idea about me," Rick drawled amiably, trying hard not to imagine how an unclothed Caroline would look in that huge four-poster bed, her naked body sprawled between silk sheets. Or how that curvy little body of hers would feel beneath his.

"Relax." Caroline interrupted Rick curtly. "This isn't what you think. I'm not coming on to you."

"You're not?" She had hair the color of bittersweet chocolate, worn in loose tousled, shoulder-length curls, flawless golden skin, thick lashed hazel eyes and perfect red bow-shaped lips. She had a willowy figure with perfect breasts and slender hips that the fitted bodice of her dress outlined to perfection. And the only thing unexpected about her to-the-manor-born-appearance was her double-pierced ears. She was wearing diamonds and gold at her throat, on her wrist, her hands, in her ears. She was still clearly spoiled and stubborn and right now, driven to succeed. The only problem was he didn't know quite what she was trying to succeed at—save puzzle and intrigue the hell out of him. And that she was doing damn well.

"No, I'm not trying to seduce you!" Color poured into the high sculpted planes of her cheeks. "I'm just playing a prank. And you have to help me. But don't worry. I'll make it worth your while. I'll pay you an extra two hundred dollars."

Rick sized her up. He'd been used by women before but never to pleasant results. The fact she was willing to pay him so much made him wary. His green eyes narrowed. "This wouldn't happen to be an old boyfriend, would it? One with a temper and a shotgun bolted to the back window of his BMW?"

"Nope." Caroline grinned and flounced toward the bed. Pausing only long enough to step over the trail of lacy undergarments that led to her private bath, she bent to rumple the covers to look as if they'd been slept in, then dashed back to his side. She frowned as her hazel-eyed gaze rested on the cheap white tuxedo coat and plain black bow tie all the caterers wore. "We've got to do something about that jacket. And that tie!" She quickly divested him of both. She wadded up the clothes and tossed them into the hope chest at the end of her bed, then slammed it shut.

"Wait here." She sped out of the room, returning with a black tuxedo jacket looped over one arm. "Put this on."

Rick allowed her to help him shrug into the jacket only because he wanted to see where this was all leading. He felt like a Ken doll getting dressed for a date.

"It's a little tight across the shoulders, but it'll do," she said finally.

"For what?" Rick asked.

Before she could answer, the sound of a car door slamming sent Caroline flying to the window. Looking down, she placed both hands on her stomach and sucked in a quick breath. "There she is."

"There who is?" Rick asked.

Caroline shut her eyes. "My mother," she said in a tormented whisper.

"Marjorie Lord, the movie star?" Rick snapped to attention as he thought of the two-time Oscar winner, who, as she approached sixty, was still one of the world's greatest beauties.

"One and the same," Caroline retorted.

"This is going to be some party."

"You can't even begin to imagine," Caroline said dryly. She rushed back to his side again. "Okay, this is what I want you to do." She spoke quickly as she unbuttoned the first three buttons on his starched white shirt with a sure, deft touch. "When my mother comes up the stairs, gaze at me and look lovingly into my eyes, like we're having these big romantic feelings or something. And then just play along with whatever I say."

Normally, Rick didn't act like a puppet on a string for anyone. In this case, since he'd sneaked in here to extract something from Caroline, he supposed he could go along with her scheme— whatever it was. Just temporarily, long enough to get his foot in the door.

"Now!" Caroline whispered, tilting her head back and linking her arms around his neck. "Kiss me!"

"Kiss you?"

"That's right!" she demanded, already cupping the back of his head with her hand and bringing his mouth down to hover above hers. "Kiss me!"

Deciding this was one princess who'd been in the driver's seat long enough, Rick grinned back at her wickedly, a plan of his own already forming in his mind. "If duty calls..." he drawled, deciding to give Caroline Lord her money's worth.

Caroline's hazel eyes widened at the low masculine promise in his voice. Not one to do *anything* halfway, he bent her backward from the waist and lowered his mouth.

And there, everything predictable about this crazy ploy of hers stopped. He'd expected her lips to be soft. He hadn't expected them to taste quite so good or be quite so giving. From her headstrong impulsive actions, he'd expected her to be part girl, but she was all woman.

Dimly, Rick heard a male voice saying in a loud, intrusive tone, "I told you we shouldn't have come up here, Mother! I told you Caroline had..." Tony cleared his throat delicately "uh...company."

Recognizing his cue for what it was, Rick slowly and deliberately lifted his mouth from Caroline's. Deciding to go for maximum effect, he made no move to let her right herself. Still bent backward from the waist, Caroline had no choice but to cling to his broad shoulders for balance. As he stared into her eyes, he realized something else. He didn't want to let her go. What he wanted was another kiss, this one deeper and more searing, more intimate, than the last. And damn her, if she didn't seem to want it, too.

"Caroline?" Marjorie asked, stunned.

Caroline turned her head and sent her mother an apologetic smile. Rick felt her tremble in his arms. He heard her struggle for breath.

"Mother," Caroline said weakly, pretending to be caught flagrante delicto and playing up the moment for all it was worth, though Rick suspected it was no chore for Caroline to look guilty and embarrassed for having been caught indulging in white-hot kisses.

Marjorie Lord's look of concern turned to a smile of satisfaction. "Aren't you going to introduce me to your beau?"

Rick had to give Caroline Lord credit. She didn't show the slightest bit of unease, even though she hadn't the foggiest idea who he really was, or why he was really here. Righting her gently, he kept his left arm around her waist and extended his right hand to her mother. "Rick Cassidy," he said. "And there's no need to tell me who you are. I've been watching you in movies—and loving you—since I was knee-high."

Marjorie smiled. "Why, thank you, Rick. It's nice to know I still have an audience out there."

Beside him, Caroline stiffened and catapulted out of his grasp. She smoothed her taffeta skirt. "You really should have let me know you were coming, Mother. Rick and I could have—" Caroline paused to draw in a deep breath "—arranged something much more intimate had we known."

What could have been more intimate? Rick wondered, his fantasies raging all the hotter. To be caught in her bed?

"As it is—"

Marjorie interrupted with a wave. "Darling, you don't have to apologize. I love parties. And as for getting to know Rick, tonight is a splendid opportunity. And I told you when we spoke on the phone a few minutes ago, I'm not leaving Houston again until you are happily married."

Now this was getting interesting, Rick thought. "Inquiring minds want to know," he whispered under his breath.

Caroline colored but kept her eyes on Marjorie. "Mother, please—" she said. "Not in front of Rick."

"On the contrary, Caroline," Rick interjected. "As your *beau,* I'd *love* to hear what your mother has to say."

Caroline pivoted, planted a hand square in the middle of his chest and gave him a steely look. "It's nothing we haven't gone over before, Rick darling." She pushed the words through a row of even white teeth. Her look said she meant business.

What she didn't know, was that so did he.

"I think she's spending far too much time chasing after the presidency of Maxwell Lord Cosmetics," Marjorie said.

Caroline pushed away from Rick restlessly and strode across the room, her petticoats rustling. "Someone has to take care of the family company, Mother," she said hotly. "And we both know the board of directors thinks Tony's the perfect man for the job just because he is a man and therefore *somehow* more stable. What they don't know is that Tony doesn't have the single-mindedness needed to run Maxwell Lord Cosmetics for the next thirty years, never mind the willingness to put in eighty-hour weeks."

"You may have a point there, sis," Tony agreed solemnly. "There'd be no time for partying if I worked *all* the time. Although in the short run," he teased, working to lighten the tensions that had sprung up in the room, "you've got to admit that it'd be an excellent way for me to meet women. Company presidencies always impress."

"So do jets," Caroline quipped as she plopped down on the unmade covers of her bed. "So why not just take flying lessons?"

"I like the idea of running the company," Tony said.

"So do I," Caroline retorted flatly. "The difference is I will put all my energy into it."

Her mother continued, "Darling, how many times do I have to tell you? The company is not going to make you happy. Settling down and making a home with a man you love will make you happy."

"Mother, ple-e-e-e-a-s-e!" Caroline massaged her temples.

"Never fear," Marjorie continued. "I'm here. And I'm going to help you get your life back on track once and for all if it's the last thing I do."

Caroline looked as if dread were spiraling through her in white-hot waves. Although he was curious to know more, Rick struggled with the urge to hightail it out of there. He had come here tonight because he'd already been turned down by Hugh Bradford and Tony Lord—who to Rick's irritation didn't even seem to remember him! He hadn't even been able to get an appointment to see Caroline Lord at all. But he hadn't bargained on finding himself immediately embroiled in their family tensions.

"How exactly do you plan to help me?" Caroline was asking her mother.

"By finding you a husband, of course," Marjorie said.

"You're serious," Caroline surmised grimly as she watched her mother work off her gloves and slip out of her mink.

"Absolutely." Marjorie returned Caroline's aggrieved look with a steely one of her own. "Not that I haven't given you plenty of time to take care of this yourself, but let's face it, darling, if you haven't found someone by the time you're thirty—"

"I'm twenty-nine," Caroline stated flatly as she rose to her feet.

"Only for one more month," Marjorie said. "Then you will be thirty. Then, Caroline, it will have been ten years since that other...incident. Long past time for you to put it behind you."

"I *have* put it behind me," Caroline said.

"Oh, really? Then why haven't you been married since..." Marjorie looked at Rick. "Since...you know."

No, he didn't, Rick thought, but he'd sure *like* to know.

"If I haven't been seriously involved," Caroline retorted hotly, "it's because I didn't *want* to be seriously involved."

Which was her absolute right, Rick thought, understanding Caroline perfectly. Relationships took too much effort and energy. Business-minded people such as Caroline and himself didn't have time for that. Not when they had their own empires to build—in his case, and run—in hers.

"I think what Mother's trying to say is she's afraid you're going to turn into a spinster. And being the hopeless romantic she is, she's here to prevent it," Tony said.

"Thanks heaps for the interpretation." Caroline shot Tony a dark look.

A flash of guilt appeared on Marjorie's face. She crossed to her daughter and took Caroline's hand in hers. "I know in the past I've been somewhat remiss in my duties as your mother," she protested softly.

"No, you haven't," Caroline said, withdrawing her hands from her mother's imploring hold. "I could do without the meddling that always comes when you're trying to help. And—"

Marjorie held up a heavily bejeweled hand, silencing her daughter. "It seems as if every time you've had a crisis, I've had to run off to do a movie or a play. But this time is going to be different, darling," she promised.

"Different? How?" Caroline interrupted wryly. "Because you're stepping in to actually *cause* the turmoil this time?"

"No," Marjorie corrected. "Different, because I mean to help you mend that fragile heart of yours. I've given the situation a lot of thought, and I really think a man is the answer."

"Don't you always!" Caroline let out a long, exasperated breath.

"Moreover, I'm going to begin scouting the eligible men in this city and help you find a husband every bit as wonderful and exciting as you are," Marjorie continued energetically.

Rick had only to look at Marjorie's face to know Caroline's mother meant every crazy word she said. And in a way he understood, even if life wasn't the movie-set drama Caroline's mother apparently thought it was. If some man *had* broken Caroline's heart...well, it *was* a shame.

"It's sweet of you to worry about me, but as you can see, I'm already dating someone." Caroline sent Rick a million-dollar smile.

"Yes, I know," Marjorie repeated impatiently. "Mr. Tall, Dark and Handsome."

"Yes, but not only him," Caroline said quickly. "I'm dating others, as well."

"Who?" Marjorie demanded.

Caroline smiled and lifted her slender shoulders in a triumphant shrug. "Hugh Bradford, for one."

Marjorie looked aghast. "That stuffy old vice president?"

Rick felt a similar surge of emotion. Hugh Bradford was a self-absorbed twit with all the business vision of an ant.

"Hugh's not old." Caroline defended herself with admirable restraint. "He's only forty-two. Rick here is—"

"Thirty-three, and your mother's right, Caroline. Hugh is too old for you." He grinned at Caroline and with a mischievous wink added, "You need someone spry enough to keep up with you."

"I suppose you're referring to yourself?" Caroline asked sweetly.

Rick liked the tartness in Caroline's voice almost as much as the sparkle in her eyes. He never had been able to resist a challenge. "I didn't hear any complaints a few minutes ago."

"I like him, Caroline!" Marjorie said.

"Well, I—"

Rick was sure Caroline was about to say "don't like him!" when she cut off her sentence abruptly.

"So, Rick—" Marjorie turned back to him with a big smile "—let's cut the social amenities and get down to brass tacks. Just how serious are you about my daughter?"

Caroline had been to hell and back when she was twenty. And all because of a man. She wasn't going to go there again. "Mother, please—" she snapped icily.

"That's a good question," Rick drawled. "But a little hard to answer at the moment."

I'll say, Caroline thought. She had "drafted" Rick from the kitchen and kissed him just to prove to her mother that she had a personal life, but she had never dreamed this half devil, half angel of a man would be so hard to handle.

"It seems as if we just met," Rick continued affably, looking gallantly determined to rescue her from this mess. "And on the other hand—" Rick stepped closer, wrapped a proprietary arm around her and gave her waist a squeeze. "I think I know her type of woman all too well."

Caroline had the uneasy feeling Rick's words weren't quite as complimentary as they sounded. Worse, her stomach was still doing flip-flops, her skin tingling, her mouth watering...and all just because of a little staged kiss. What had gotten into her anyway? She'd been kissed before. Plenty of times! Men didn't affect her this way, making her feel all soft and sexy and weak in the knees!

"'Her type'?" Marjorie finally asked.

"You know," Rick answered, his voice as captivating as his smile. "Driven. Career-oriented. Hard to get ahold of."

Caroline was sure even her mother could hear the double edge his words had. Really, the man was taking his role-playing too far! "You're hardly ordinary, Rick," Caroline said sweetly.

She suddenly wished she hadn't picked him out of the men crowding her kitchen. But Rick Cassidy was drop-dead handsome, with soft, thick jet-black hair that was too long by current standards. It brushed his collar and the tops of his ears in pleasantly shaggy, tousled layers. His eyes were a dark forest green. He had a sexy smile and a swaggering, all-male gait that suggested he didn't take trouble from anyone. And he towered over her. But it was more than just his height that had her in awe; it was the sheer dwarfing width of his shoulders, the washboard flatness of his stomach and chest, the wealth of tight economical muscle in his lean hips and long legs. He looked more rancher than caterer.

Still, noticing his firm, square don't-mess-with-me jaw, and his tan, she was even more certain she was not dealing with any ordinary city slicker. Just who she was dealing with? Now that she took the time to study him, he looked familiar to her. Had she seen his picture somewhere? In the papers maybe? She knew she hadn't met him personally. She'd recall if she had.

Rick was grinning down at her insolently. "You sure make me feel special, princess," he drawled.

Caroline extricated herself from the tantalizing warmth of his arm. She regretted her own foolhardy impetuousness almost as much as she now distrusted him. "Don't call me that," she commanded bad-temperedly.

"Can't help it, princess. You're just so spirited and pretty."

She glared at him. "Mother, if you'll excuse us a moment." Clasping his wrist, she dragged him behind a Chinese dressing screen. Unfortunately, her clothes were scattered here, as well. Rick picked up a lacy camisole and held it to his face before she could stop him.

"Nice perfume," he said, breathing in deeply. He gave her a wicked smile, as if he couldn't resist teasing her. "Smells exactly like you. All flowery."

Caroline blushed fiercely and snatched it back. "Look, Rick," she warned, "if you want to stay in my good graces, you better stop clowning around and play this prank exactly the way I want it played. And that means no more improvising!" *No more kissing her with red-hot intensity!*

Without warning, Rick put his arms out on either side of her, so her back was flat against the wall and her breasts pressed against the unyielding surface of his chest. Her petticoats and silk taffeta dress were squished in between them. "What makes you think I want to play at all?" he asked, his thick straight brows lifting over his narrowed green eyes.

Feeling as if she'd just grabbed an irascible tiger by the tail, Caroline squared her shoulders and drew herself up to her full five-foot-six height and prepared to do battle.

"Careful," Rick warned, his glance taking in the bare curves of her shoulders and the sparkling diamond necklace at her throat before returning with sensual deliberation to her eyes. He stared at her with taunting intensity. "Anything above a whisper and your mother and Tony are bound to hear."

Suffused with heat everywhere his eyes had touched, Caroline swallowed. She wished fervently she had elected to wear anything else but this fire-engine-red dress, with its drop sleeves and bosom-revealing sweetheart neckline. She forced herself to take a calming breath. "You agreed to do anything you could to help me, Rick. I expect you to honor that agreement."

Slowly he lowered his face to hers. His eyes glittered hungrily. "Maybe I didn't know what I was getting into."

Neither did I, Caroline thought. She struggled to remember the point of all this—which was to get her mother off her back about having a satisfying love life. "All you have to do from this point forward, is keep your mouth shut and agree with everything I say."

Rick leaned forward. As he did so, his lips touched her temple. "How can I agree if I have my mouth shut?"

Fighting the electric heat his touch had elicited, Caroline regarded him icily. She should have known by the confident, controlled way he held himself that Rick was the kind of man who would never be satisfied unless he held the upper hand. "It's simple. You nod." She pushed the words through gritted teeth, finding it an effort to hang on to her legendary cool.

Rick only made a *tsk*ing sound and grinned from ear to ear. He dropped one hand from the wall and lifted her chin. "Is this the way you treat all your men friends? If so, it's no wonder you're not married." Still gazing deep into her eyes, he curved his hand around her cheek and chin. "But then again, maybe you just haven't met the right man."

He hadn't even tried to kiss her again, though he could have, and was merely touching her face, yet Caroline's nipples tightened almost painfully beneath her lacy red Merry Widow corset. Lower still, there was a definite pressure building, a new weakness in her knees. And the renewed desire to experience his kiss.... This was crazy, she thought, drawing in a shaky breath. She was not the kind of woman who could ever be swept off her feet. Not anymore. Not since...

Caroline jerked her face away from his hand. "Cut that out."

"Sorry," Rick said.

But he wasn't, Caroline thought, as she propped both her hands on the cinched waist of her dress. "Are you going to cooperate with me, or do I throw you out of here summarily?"

"And explain it how?" he demanded lazily as he probed her eyes.

"Lovers' quarrel!" she shot back. Lovers' quarrels didn't have to make sense. Lovers' quarrels ran on emotion—something she was feeling plenty of. And, according to the parameters of good taste, didn't have to be explained.

"Caroline, really!" Marjorie called. "You and Rick come out from behind that screen this instant!"

Caroline decided her only recourse with Rick was to take a firm stand. Just as she did in business. "Remember, if you don't behave, you're out of here," she warned.

He straightened enough to allow her to pass, then shrugged. "Seems to me *you're* in more trouble than *I* am if I don't behave."

Unfortunately, that was true. Caroline shot him an aggrieved look over her shoulder. It was for this reason exactly she dreaded getting involved with men. They made life so unnecessarily complicated.

"Darling, please. Your guests are arriving!"

"Maybe you all should go down and greet them for us," Caroline suggested. She took Rick's hand firmly in hers and drew him out into the center of the room.

"Right," Rick finished smoothly. He let go of her hand, wrapped an arm about her waist and tugged her close. "Caroline and I still have some things to work out."

To Caroline's immense irritation, her mother seemed to be liking Rick more every minute. The more unmanageable he got, the more her mother liked him. Which figured, Caroline thought. Unlike Caroline, there was nothing Marjorie liked more than having a masterful man come in and take charge of her life.

"You still didn't answer my question," Marjorie reminded. "Just how serious are you about my daughter?"

Rick looked at Caroline, staring deep into her eyes. "Very serious," he said.

"And Caroline?" Marjorie persisted. "How do you feel about Rick? Come along, Tony," she said, when Caroline didn't answer right away. "It's time to begin looking for a new beau for your sister."

"Now wait just a minute, Mother. I can't believe you would actually husband hunt for me!" Caroline groaned.

Marjorie shrugged. "I simply won't rest until I know you have someone to keep you warm at night."

Rick grinned. "I know exactly how you feel, Marjorie," he quipped with feigned sympathy. "I don't think I'm going to rest, either."

Tony doubled over with laughter. Caroline thought of the perfect diversion. "Why not marry *him* off?" She pointed to her brother.

"I plan to," Marjorie promised with a smile. "As soon as I take care of you."

"In that case, Mother, you may as well know." Caroline released a beleaguered sigh, to great theatrical effect. "I'm very serious about Rick, too." *Serious about keeping him in line.*

"Serious enough to marry him?" Marjorie probed softly.

Caroline didn't want to play this game but her mother had forced her into it. Like it or not, it was time to fish or cut bait. "Yes," she said. She quickly qualified her statement with the words she'd use to bail herself out of this mess later, after she'd won the Maxwell Lord Presidency permanently. "But only when the time is right."

Chapter Two

"That was some performance," Rick drawled. "Does she know she's not the only actress in the family?"

"Would you shut up? I have to think." Caroline hurried to her vanity. What she saw in her mirror didn't please her. Her hazel eyes were unnaturally bright, her skin unnaturally pale. Her lower lip was bare and trembling. She picked up a tube of Maxwell Lord's Ravishing Red and began to apply it to her mouth.

Rick strolled over to observe. He propped himself against the wall and crossed his arms over his chest. Where the jacket of the Armani tux was too tight, it bunched around his shoulders and armpits. And yet the overall effect—of starched white shirt and black jacket—against the golden tan of his skin and the midnight black of his hair was devastating.

He peered at her closely. "I think you're right. I think a little lipstick would help. You might try some rouge, too."

Caroline shot him an aggrieved look. With the tip of her finger, she dabbed at a smudge of lipstick on one corner of her lip and purposefully ignored the compact of Ravishing Red blush on her vanity. "Believe me, if I could get rid of you now," she informed him with icy disdain, glueing her eyes to her reflection in the mirror, "I would."

"But you can't, can you?" Rick tilted his head, watching raptly as she outlined the upper bow of her lip in the exact shade of fire-engine-red as her pretty dress. "Not after that charming little display you just put on for Marjorie."

"Stop reminding me," Caroline snapped. She couldn't believe the bad timing. Her mother arriving on the evening of the most important business dinner of her life!

"Someone has to remind you," Rick said without rancor. He dragged a chair over, turned it around backward and sat down on it with his folded arms resting on the back. "What's this all about, anyway?" He rested his chin on a propped up fist and waited patiently for her to reply. "I am assuming of course that you don't draft make-believe fiancés for yourself every day."

"Of course I don't. And we're not engaged. Just serious enough to contemplate marriage."

"Right." Rick nodded at her with mock solemnity. "I stand corrected." His dark green gaze narrowed. "That still doesn't explain why you're going to such great lengths to pacify your mother. Why not just tell her to bug off?"

Caroline's posture was as stiff and unyielding as her mood. She whirled to face him. "I have. Numerous times. It doesn't work. She's romantic to the core. She can't get it through her head that I am not miserable because I don't have a man dancing attendance on me night and day."

The corner of his mouth lifted in a smile. "Have you *ever* had a man dancing attendance on you night and day?"

Not like you would, Rick Cassidy, Caroline thought, then, uncomfortable with the images coming quickly to mind—Rick sweeping her into his arms, running his hands through her hair, kissing her hotly—pushed the thoughts away. "No," she said stiffly. "Nor would I want it."

"Ah." Rick paused and nodded gravely, like a professor studying his subject. "Back to your mother..."

"If she starts playing matchmaker she's going to embarrass me in front of all my colleagues."

"The people downstairs?"

"Yes. Tonight is a business dinner. I've invited all the members of the board of directors of the company where I work—"

"Maxwell Lord Cosmetics," Rick supplied, following the enormously complicated situation with alarming alacrity.

Caroline narrowed her eyes suspiciously. "How do you know so much about me?"

Rick lifted his broad shoulders in a shrug. "Everyone in Houston knows about the beautiful Caroline Lord. You're in the paper at least once a week. As is your charming but somewhat ne'er-do-well brother, Tony."

Abruptly aware her hand was trembling, Caroline recapped her lipstick tube and put it on her vanity table. There was too much stress in her life at the moment. That was the problem. Her trembling had nothing whatsoever to do with Rick and the way he had kissed her or the fact they were now talking in her bedroom like two old friends...or the fact that he knew far more about her than she felt comfortable with.

She dropped her hand casually and hid it in the folds of her dress. "You read the society page?"

Rick's eyes lit up wickedly. "When you're on it, I sure do."

The man was trouble all right, with a capital T. And she should have realized it sooner.

Pretending an ease she couldn't begin to feel, Caroline picked up a brush and raked it through the thick unruly waves of her dark brown hair. "Look, if you're thinking I shouldn't have nabbed you like that and offered to pay you to pretend to be romantically interested in me, you're right."

Rick stood and swaggered over, so he was beside her. He let his eyes trail over her slowly. "I'm not complaining, princess. I enjoyed kissing you. I enjoyed it a lot."

That was the problem. So had she. "Stop calling me princess!" Caroline warned.

His eyes glinted appreciatively, but he made no argument.

"Unfortunately," Caroline continued, willing her pounding heart to slow its frantic pace, "now that my mother's picked up the gauntlet, there's no way out of it. We're just going to have to brazen our way through this evening."

"Fine with me."

"Why am I not surprised by that?" Caroline muttered to herself before disappearing down the hall. She returned moments later with a black silk bow tie she'd borrowed from Tony's closet and tossed it at him.

Rick caught it with one hand and laced it around his neck. "Don't look so worried," he advised.

"That's easy for you to say," Caroline retorted. He wasn't trying to gain the company presidency from a room full of men who seemed to want nothing more than to award the presidency to someone else.

Rick studied her with misgiving. "You think your mother suspects we're not really interested in one another?" he asked as he tied.

Caroline spritzed herself with perfume then calmly put down the glass bottle. "Wouldn't you?"

Rick finished tying his bow tie, then looked at her in the mirror. "Maybe we could be more convincing," he said, looking forward to the prospect with obvious relish.

Caroline didn't know what could be more convincing than his kiss. She also knew her mother was no fool. If Marjorie thought for a moment Caroline was yanking her chain, there'd be no telling how she might retaliate. And the most likely way would be to campaign against Caroline in the race for company presidency. If Marjorie did that, there was no doubt in Caroline's mind that either Hugh or Tony would be named president in her stead. It wouldn't matter that Caroline could do a better job.

Ignoring Rick's closeness and the delicious way he smelled, she leaned closer to the mirror and replaced two of the diamond studs in her ears with diamond drop earrings.

"Look, just behave yourself this evening, okay? This is a business dinner. Conduct yourself accordingly. And as for how we know each other, I'll just introduce you to my co-workers as a friend." She paused, clamping her lips together. "Will any of the caterers give you away?"

Rick smiled. "I'll ask them not to."

"Good." Aware he was being almost too cooperative now, when just moments earlier he'd been doing everything he could to tease her and thwart her plans, she shot him a suspicious look. "You're not going to let me down, are you?"

"I'll do whatever you want," Rick promised.

Caroline studied him but could find nothing untrustworthy in his face. It was funny. She usually took a long time to warm up to men. Especially roguishly attractive men near her own age. And yet from the moment she'd laid eyes on Rick, she'd felt peculiarly drawn to him. Interested in some fundamental way.

He buttoned his jacket and offered her his arm. "Ready to go down?"

At least he knew how to behave like a gentleman. "I guess we'd better."

Rick grinned, looking far happier than he had a right to be. Caroline's skin prickled uncomfortably. She knew next to nothing about this man, even if he did look...familiar. "Don't look so pleased with yourself," she warned. "The evening is not over yet."

"So how did the two of you meet?" Hugh Bradford asked the moment Caroline and Rick sat down to dinner.

Caroline resisted the urge to squirm in her chair as her balding, bespectacled colleague regarded her with frank personal interest. She and Hugh had dated off and on the past six years. More often than not, the confirmed bachelor escorted her to company and social functions. But there had never been anything the least bit sexual between them, and probably never would be. He was more like a brother to her, the kind of nurturing, overprotective older brother Tony might have been had he not been such a playboy himself. Lately, though, there'd been a definite strain in their relationship, since they were both vying for the company presidency.

"It's a long story," Caroline finally said, taking a sip of her champagne.

"Tell us anyway, darling," Marjorie prodded.

"Yeah," Tony said, prodding Caroline deliberately and reminding her that he also knew what she was up to with Rick. "I'd like to hear this myself."

Thanks a lot, big brother. "Well—" she hedged. She looked at Rick.

"It was at a party," he said, jumping to her rescue.

"When?" demanded Miriam Humphrey, the only other female executive in Maxwell Lord. The fifty-year-old woman was as stuffy as she was sharp, having preferred to spend most of her time in the labs cooking up new skin-care products with the other chemists.

"Gosh..." Caroline said, pretending to think. "It was a while back."

Rick smiled at her and added smoothly, "Though it seems like we've known each other forever."

"Funny, you never mentioned Rick to me," Hugh murmured with a decidedly proprietary frown in Caroline's direction.

"Caroline likes to keep her private life private," Rick said.

"I certainly do," Caroline affirmed with a deliberate smile at the group assembled at her dinner table.

"So what do you do, Rick?" Tony asked.

Rick grinned and leaned back in his chair. "Mostly manage my investments, though I do have a few new projects on the back burner." He turned to Caroline with a meaningful look only she could see. "Looks like they're going to heat up sooner than I thought."

"But enough about us," Caroline said quickly, fighting the heat that threatened to rise to her face. "The reason I brought you all here tonight was to talk about the company presidency."

"I may as well tell you," Caroline's mother interjected, "I'm against Caroline taking over the presidency. Not that she hasn't done a wonderful job running it since Max died, but—Caroline, that's no life for you."

"I beg to differ with you, Mother," she said with a calm and confident smile. "It's precisely the life for me."

"You think so now. But when those eighteen-hour days start adding up over time, you'll never have time to find yourself a husband."

The members of the board chuckled. Caroline pretended to be amused, but inwardly, she wondered if things could get much worse. "I thought we had discussed this, Mother," she said pleasantly.

"Your mother has a point, Caroline," Hugh interjected kindly. "The job of president is very demanding. What happens if you do marry and want to have a child?"

"Then I will," Caroline said impatiently, resenting the implication she couldn't do both simultaneously, if she chose.

"It's true that recent studies have shown that married people make better executives. Maybe because they're more stable. But suppose your husband works on the West Coast?" Cy Rutledge, the head of advertising, intervened. "Would you expect everyone here to relocate there for your convenience?"

"No, of course not," Caroline said, losing patience with the aging board and their hopelessly outdated ideas on women and marriage. "He'd have to move."

"And you think that would be a workable compromise, as far as your husband would be concerned?" Cy continued.

"I'm sure it would be." Rick jumped in with both feet. "No offense, gentlemen, Marjorie, Ms. Humphrey, but the needs of the modern man are definitely changing. No one my age expects his wife to stay home and do the dishes while he goes out and brings home the bacon. Couples these days both work. Both jobs take priority. Both spouses make sacrifices in that regard." Rick gave Caroline a steady look, laced with confidence in her ability. "I am sure whatever happens, that Caroline would see to it that her work did not suffer in the slightest."

Caroline sent Rick a grateful glance. "What's important here are my plans for Maxwell Lord. I'd like to introduce a new line of makeup and skin-care products, geared strictly for the young teen, featuring lots of lip glosses and pale translucent colors the girls will love and their mothers will approve of.''

"Wait a minute," Tony said, looking aggrieved she hadn't consulted him before introducing her idea to the board. "That sounds like a lot of work, Caroline, for an uncertain market."

"Tony's right," Hugh said quickly. "You know our market research has always shown that girls that age buy their cosmetics at the drugstore."

"Only because they can't buy them in the department store," Caroline argued.

"Girls that age don't have a lot of extra cash to spend," Cy Rutledge intervened.

"Their mothers do," Caroline said. "Besides, we'll offer services like free makeovers and skin analysis and consultation that the girls can't get at the drugstores. Their mothers will love that, because when they leave our counter, they will look fresh and pretty in a barely made-up way, instead of like some little girl playing dress-up with her mommy's cosmetics."

"Well, I for one would welcome the challenge," Miriam Humphrey said. "Most of my work to date has been geared to antiaging. Young skin presents different challenges, but I'm sure we could come up with products that would work to discourage and perhaps even prevent excess oiliness and breakouts.''

Caroline smiled at their senior chemist. ''Thank you, Miriam,'' she said.

Miriam beamed.

''I still think it's an awfully big risk,'' Hugh cut in. As he was the head of marketing, everyone turned to him, listening intently. ''We're not just talking product-development costs here, Caroline, but marketing and advertising, as well.''

''I'm aware of that, Hugh. But think of the potential rewards!''

''If it pans out,'' Hugh said. ''You have to remember,'' he continued, ''the company is still in transition. Since Max died last year, there's been no single visible spokesperson for the company. Oh, I know Caroline's taken over the new store openings at the malls. I've handled the *Business Week* interviews, and Tony's handled all the shipping, but it's not the same as when Max was in charge.''

''Precisely why I should be named president,'' Caroline said. ''I'm not only family. I have ideas for the future growth of Maxwell Lord, just like Dad did.''

''Still, the company has always been associated with the image of a man,'' Cy Rutledge cut in gravely. "As far as advertising goes, Tony is still the logical first choice."

At that, Tony beamed.

"And maybe," Rick interjected, "it's time for a change. After all, Caroline's very beautiful. Maxwell Lord markets cosmetics..."

"Among other things," Hugh said, looking more unhappy than ever with the way things were going.

"What better spokesperson for a cosmetics company than a beautiful woman?" Rick continued, ignoring Hugh. "The strategy has certainly worked for Elizabeth Arden and Estée Lauder."

"Our competitors!" Hugh exclaimed huffily, as if even mentioning the two women was an act of absolute heresy.

"You're forgetting the most important part," Marjorie cut in. "Caroline still needs to get married. I was worried enough about her finding a husband to settle down with, as is. But with her trying to develop a new line, too..." Marjorie shook her head and leaned forward. "Darling," she implored, "trust me on this. All eight of my marriages ended in divorce because of the demands of my profession, because I had to go off on location to work. Even when I was acting on the soundstages in Hollywood, the days were incredibly long and arduous. Just as yours will be if you take this job—"

To Caroline's aggravation, the board began to look worried again. As if all her great ideas had been for naught!

Rick turned to Caroline. "I told you we should have made our announcement beforehand," he said smugly.

What announcement? Caroline thought, beginning ever so slightly to panic.

Rick took Marjorie's hand in his. "Caroline doesn't need to worry about finding a husband who is understanding about the demands of her job."

"She doesn't?" Marjorie asked, confused.

"No," Rick continued smoothly before Caroline could get a word in edgewise. "Caroline and I are engaged."

"I CANNOT BELIEVE you did that to me!" Caroline stormed the moment they were alone. She'd waited as long as she could, but cut out with Rick, shortly after they had finished dessert, leaving her mother and Tony to entertain the group gathered around their piano.

Rick shrugged. "It cut off the talk about husband hunting. I thought that was what you wanted."

Caroline shut the doors to the library firmly, blocking out the faint sounds of Tony's piano playing and her mother's celebrated voice. "Don't you understand what you've done?'' she asked, then went straight to the desk, removed two hundred dollars and promptly paid him.

Rick's eyes held hers as he pocketed the money. ''Yeah. I got your matchmaking mother off your back. And that had to be done, princess. Because she was making you look like a teenager without a date to the prom in front of all those board members.''

Caroline sighed. Whether she liked it or not, Rick had saved the day.

''Has Marjorie always been like that?'' he asked. Stepping behind her, he began to massage Caroline's shoulders. His hands were magic. Kneading. Soothing. With just the right amounts of gentleness and pressure.

Realizing she was succumbing to Rick's seductive ways again, Caroline skated away from him abruptly. ''Unfortunately, yes, she has always been like that.'' Caroline gestured lamely. ''Maybe it's because she was always off making or promoting a movie. Whenever she's with me, she always mothers me like there's no tomorrow. She wants to get everything done *today*. She doesn't want to leave with any loose ends behind her that she'll later feel guilty about. When Dad was alive, of course, he kind of worked to calm her down. She always knew he was right here, loving us and watching over us.

But since he died . . . I don't know . . . she's been in a panic, almost. Trying to make sure that Tony and I are both deliriously happy, in case anything should happen to her, too."

Rick grinned, understanding perfectly. "Mothers," he said. "They never get over feeling we need rescuing. My mother's still waiting for me to find that one special woman, just like yours is husband hunting for you."

"Unfortunately," Caroline said wryly, "I'd die before waiting around for some knight on a white charger to rescue me."

"That's a shame," Rick said. Flinging off his jacket and tie, he dropped into a nearby chair.

"What?" Caroline sat opposite him and arranged her voluminous skirts with a rustle of silk taffeta over organza.

"Your lack of romance. Given half a chance, princess, you might like the idea of being rescued. You might like it a lot."

Caroline got up to pace the room. "Give it up, Rick," she advised coolly, without a backward glance. "I've already paid you and I'm immune to sweet talk. I've spent years warding off advances from much more determined men than you."

He followed her over to the floor-to-ceiling bookshelves. His voice was hushed, seductive, his breath warm on her shoulder. "Is that what you

think I'm doing, Caroline, trying to sweet-talk
you?''

When she didn't answer, he placed his hands on
the bare curves of her shoulders and turned her to
face him. Caroline ignored the sensual feeling of his
palms on her bare skin. They were slightly rough,
callused, like he knew firsthand the value of hard
physical work, and yet tender, too, like he also
knew how to love. Irritated with herself, Caroline
wondered where that thought had come from.

"I haven't a clue as to what you're doing," she
denied hotly, with a regal toss of her head. She bit
her lip, aware he was looking like he wanted very
much to haul her against him and kiss her again, as
thoroughly and expertly as he had before. She
swallowed around the dryness in her throat. "If
you're not out to blackmail me—"

His hands followed the curve of her shoulders,
caressing her bare arms. "Cross my heart, I'm
not."

His tone was so abruptly earnest, so abruptly
forthright, she forgot what she was going to say.
Looking into his forest-green eyes, feeling the
warmth of his touch, and inhaling his rich, winter
pine scent, she could almost... almost believe he
wasn't out to hurt her. "Then what *do* you want?"

I want a lot, Rick thought. But Caroline was in
no position to help him with the business proposi-

tion he had planned to put to her tonight. She was fighting for the presidency with everything she had. Rick's only chance to see his own plans come to fruition was shot if Caroline didn't become president of Maxwell Lord. Hence, he would have to put his own plans on hold, for however long it was necessary, and help her achieve her goals first. Then, when her own position was secure, they would talk.

"I want a chance to spend time with you this next month," Rick said.

Caroline's glance narrowed, as if she knew instinctively that he had to want more than just the pleasure of her company. "Sorry. There's no way I can do that."

"There's no way you can't," Rick argued. "We're now engaged, remember? If you don't spend time with me, your mother—national theatrical treasure though she is—is liable to start husband hunting for you again."

He had a point there, Caroline thought. But as for the rest of his madcap scheme, it was impossible. "I'm going to go back in there now and tell everyone it was a joke."

"You could," Rick allowed with a shrug, letting her go. "But—"

"What?" The reservation on his face unnerved her more than she wanted to admit.

His eyes narrowed. "Don't you think you waited a tad bit too long for that?"

"They'll understand," Caroline insisted, telling herself it was so.

"They'll think you're weak," he predicted.

And impulsive to a fault, Caroline thought. She never should have pulled Rick out of the kitchen or drafted him into the role of her suitor. "So what are you proposing?" she asked warily.

"That we go along with this ruse, purposefully keep it low-key, until after you've won the company presidency and your mother has gone back to Los Angeles."

Caroline hated to admit it, but Rick's plan made sense. He'd already assured the board his views on marriage were both modern and generous. He'd openly supported her work, charmed her mother and applauded her boldness in business. As long as she was engaged, the question of her personal life would no longer be an issue, either with the board or her mother. And since the board seemed to think that married executives were more stable, her engagement would give her an edge over both Tony and Hugh.

"It won't be for long," Rick continued, working to persuade her. "The board votes on the new president in another month."

Alarm rippled through her. "How did you know that?"

"How could I not?" Rick shrugged. "It's all everyone in the Houston business community has been talking about for weeks now. With Tony and Hugh both fighting you tooth and nail for the job, you've got no choice. You made this bed." Rick sent her a crocodile grin that spoke volumes about the sensual intent of his announcement. "Now you're just going to have to lie in it."

Chapter Three

"There you are, Caroline. I thought you and Rick were never coming back out to join the party."

"Sorry, Mother, but Rick and I had a lot to discuss."

"Like the wedding date?"

"I think it should be soon," Rick said.

Caroline squared her shoulders and looked him straight in his mischievously twinkling green eyes. "I think we should wait until after the company presidency is decided."

"Well, it will have to be before I go back to Los Angeles again to start work on my new film," Marjorie declared. "And that will be in six weeks."

Everyone was looking at her. "Fine," Caroline said. What did it matter anyway, since she was never going to go through with it? And if, in the meantime, it got her mother off her back and kept her busy...

"How about February 28?" Rick said, after consulting his pocket calendar. "The vote is on February 21."

Caroline's skin prickled. How did Rick know the exact date? He'd obviously snooped into the details of her life. But why? Was it possible, could he be a spy for another company? An overly interested Maxwell Lord stockholder? Or just another fortune hunter out to snare her?

Aware everyone was waiting for her answer, Caroline said, "Fine."

Marjorie's eyes narrowed suspiciously. She knew as did everyone else in the room it wasn't like Caroline to be so easily led. "You don't even know what day of the week it is, Caroline."

Caroline looked at Rick. "I assume you chose a weekend day?"

"Saturday."

She turned back to her mother with a shrug. "See? Everything's fine."

"I'll be the judge of that," Marjorie murmured so only Caroline could hear.

One by one, the guests said good-night. Soon the only people left in the foyer were Rick, Tony, Marjorie and Caroline.

"Rick, you'll join us for breakfast tomorrow morning?" Marjorie pressed.

Rick smiled at Marjorie, seeming to like the woman as much as she liked him. "Be glad to," he said.

"If you'll excuse me, I've got to talk to the caterers." Caroline left Rick chatting politely with Tony and her mother.

Marilu, the job boss, wasn't hard to spot. "Look, I know I commandeered one of your workers tonight—" Caroline began.

Marilu removed her white chef's apron, neatly folded it and put it in one of the Gourmet Feast boxes. "That's okay. I know Rick wanted to talk to you."

Caroline blinked, confused. "You do?"

"Yes. That's why he came in with my crew. He doesn't normally work for me, but I've done a lot of jobs for him in the past. So I figured I owed him the favor, even though it does seem to be the craziest way I've ever heard of to meet a woman. But then, what do I know about how up-and-coming tycoons get dates these days? I'm an old married woman." Marilu smiled slyly. "The ploy seemed to have worked. It didn't take you long to notice Rick and invite him to join you for dinner."

"No, it didn't, did it?" Caroline murmured, feeling very much like she'd been had. How delighted Rick must have been when she commandeered him right off the bat, she thought with a heart that was sinking fast.

Still shaken by what she had just learned—this seemed to be her worst nightmare coming true—Caroline forced herself to smile and say good-night to Marilu. She headed back to the front hall. The lights were off. Her mother and Tony had both apparently already gone to bed. Rick was nowhere in sight.

She stepped out the front door. Rick was standing in the shadows, next to a gleaming white Jaguar. It had stopped raining, but the ground was still damp, the cool winter air scented with rain. Not wanting their voices to carry, she picked up her skirt with one hand, and closed the distance between them. "Is that your car?"

Rick shrugged out of the borrowed tux jacket and untied his tie. "What'd you think I'd drive?"

"I don't know." Caroline shivered as Rick placed Tony's jacket around her shoulders. The silk lining was still warm with Rick's body heat, the fabric carried his scent. Being enveloped in it, was like being enveloped in him. "I don't know anything about you," she continued, willing herself to think about the mess she'd gotten herself into, instead of how handsome and alluring Rick looked in the moonlit Texas night. "Including how or why you sneaked in here tonight."

"That's easy." He smiled down at her as he stuffed Tony's tie into the pocket of Tony's jacket. "I wanted to meet you."

"Why?"

Rick shrugged. "Considering all that's happened, it's a moot point." He sent her an openly amused look that sent her temper soaring. "Don't you think we had better be concentrating on our future?"

His teasing only served to make her angrier. "What future?" Caroline grated.

"Why, the one your mother's planning for us, of course."

Industrial spy or fortune hunter. "What do you really do for a living?" she demanded.

He regarded her with choirboy innocence. "Exactly what I said at the dinner table. Manage my investments."

If he used Marilu's catering service regularly, he had to be well-off financially, but she also knew that fact alone didn't exclude the possibility that he was just after her money. "Are you married?"

His sensual lips compressed sternly. "I wouldn't have kissed you like that or agreed to get engaged if I was."

As he stared down at her, Caroline had the sharp impression he wanted to kiss her again.

"You don't trust me, do you?" he said.

Caroline didn't hesitate. "No. I don't."

Half his mouth lifted in an approving smile. "All things given, that's probably as it should be. Good night, Caroline."

Panic set in as Caroline realized she hadn't found out anything. "Wait!"

He opened the door of his Jaguar.

"I don't even know how to reach you."

"Don't worry, princess. I'll find you."

CAROLINE SLOWLY CLIMBED the stairs to her room. Tony was waiting for her.

"I've seen you get yourself into some messes, but this takes the cake."

She tossed his jacket and tie at him. "Shut up."

"Advice you should've given yourself a couple of hours ago," Tony said, lounging on her upholstered chaise with characteristic laziness. "Claiming the guy as a current love interest was one thing. As your fiancé..."

The impact of what she'd done was just beginning to hit her. Caroline sat down on the rumpled covers of her bed. All she had wanted to do was buy herself some time, to prevent her mother from interfering in her life. At least until after she had secured the presidency of Maxwell Lord Cosmetics for herself. It would have worked, too, if Rick hadn't been so damn intent on turning the tables on her, just the way she was trying to turn them on her mother.

She looked her tormenting older brother in the eye. She knew he wouldn't turn her in. "Do you think Mother suspects?"

Tony grinned. "Yep."

"What do you think she's going to do about it?"

"Hang you out to dry if she can catch you at it."

"And if she can't?" Caroline asked.

Tony hummed "The Wedding March." Caroline took off her shoe and hurled it at him. He ducked, laughing. "Better get your rest, Caroline. I have a feeling breakfast tomorrow is going to be a humdinger."

RICK WAS SHOWN IN promptly at eight. Marjorie Lord was in the sunroom at the rear of the River Oaks mansion, a feather-trimmed negligee and peignoir spread out around her like a royal robe. He grinned at her and walked forward to give her the light peck on the cheek he was sure she expected. "I didn't know women could look so glamorous this early in the morning," he murmured.

"Most of us don't."

Rick turned in the direction of the low, sassy voice. He grinned with pleasure as a sweaty Caroline slammed in through the screen door and stomped toward him. In baggy, misshapen gray sweats and high-topped sneakers, a terry-cloth sweatband around her forehead, her mane of glorious bittersweet chocolate hair drawn up into a high, bouncy ponytail on the back of her head, she was the antithesis of her glamorous, movie-star mother. And yet all-woman just the same.

She bounded into a wicker settee and shot Rick a smug look. He'd expected her to be as baffled and wary as she had been when he'd left last night. Apparently the seven hours they'd had apart had given her ample time to recover.

"Howdy, fella," she drawled with an impudent grin.

Rick didn't know why, but this morning Caroline was throwing herself into the role of his fiancée with enthusiasm. For Marjorie's benefit?

"Hi, yourself." He ambled on over to the settee and sat down beside her, making sure they were so close, their thighs were touching. He stretched his arm out along the back of the seat. Ignoring the almost imperceptible way she stiffened at his touch, he gave Caroline a kiss on her brow and tasted both the salt of her sweat and the deliciously sweet tang of her skin.

"A fella's gotta get up mighty early in the morning to catch you," he remarked lazily.

Caroline turned and gazed deeply into his eyes. "And even then," she finished sweetly, "he might not do so."

"All right, you two. Save the billing and cooing for later," Marjorie said, rolling up her sleeves. "We have a wedding to plan." She picked up a note pad and pen.

Caroline bounded to her feet and headed to the crystal decanter of orange juice. She poured herself an enormous glass. "Must we do this right now?"

"Yes, as a matter of fact, we must," Marjorie insisted.

Caroline paced back and forth, gulping her orange juice. She had a lot to do at the office. She didn't want this engagement business taking up a lot of her time. "You know, Rick, maybe we should elope. It'd be a lot simpler."

"Over my dead body," Marjorie declared. "You'll not do what you did the last—"

Last time? Rick thought. He hadn't read anything about Caroline being married before and he had researched her thoroughly.

"Okay, okay." Caroline hastily cut her mother off.

Marjorie's eyes narrowed. "Rick doesn't know, does he?"

Caroline sent her mother a censuring glance. "How many times have you told me a lady has to have some secrets?"

"But, Caroline—" Marjorie protested.

"No buts." Caroline ignored Rick's curious look. Additional color sprang into her cheeks. "The subject is closed," she continued. "As is our getting married in the church. We'll have it... outside. In the backyard."

Marjorie looked skeptical. "It could rain."

"If it does, we'll set up tents," Caroline reassured her quickly. "It'll be fabulous, Mother. You'll see."

"We need engagement pictures," Rick said.

Both women turned to face him. Marjorie looked pleased with his thoughtfulness. Caroline was impatient. "Why?"

Proving himself to be every bit the accomplished actor she was when backed into a corner, Rick's eyes held hers with a look that was all innocence. "Something tells me I'm going to want to remember the next few weeks the rest of my life," he drawled.

Caroline sent him a sharp look her mother couldn't see. "I have a feeling we're both going to recall this in vivid detail," she said dryly. "So vivid, in fact, we won't even need pictures."

"Oh, yes we do," Marjorie interjected. She turned to her future son-in-law. "I think it's a marvelous idea, Rick. Did you have any special photographer in mind?"

"As a matter of fact, yes." Rick smiled. "I've already taken the liberty of hiring him. Mario Shapello's flying in from New York. He'll be here tonight."

Caroline did a double take. "*The* Mario Shapello?"

"Only the best for you, princess."

Caroline finished her juice in a single gulp. She still had to shower and get to the office. "I've got a meeting tonight."

"Then free yourself," Rick said. This was important. Even if she didn't yet grasp how important. He had a plan for helping make her indispensable to her family company. And once that happened, they'd both get what they wanted.

"Rick—"

"I went to a lot of trouble and expense to hire him, princess." Rick gave Caroline a warning look.

"All right," Caroline capitulated reluctantly.

Marjorie clapped her hands together. "This will be marvelous."

"Won't it?" Rick agreed, deadpan, thinking the two women didn't know the half of what was about to happen. "He'll be here at seven." He looked at

Caroline, who was busy tugging her mane of hair from its restrictive ponytail. His mouth went dry as he watched her shake her hair free. She looked good like that. Damn good. He forced his mind back to business. "Shall I arrange for a hairdresser for the shoot or would you like to do your own?"

"Maybe I'll go as is," Caroline said sweetly, pulling her sweaty headband down past her nose and catching it between her teeth. "Show the world what kind of wife you're really getting."

"Caroline!" Marjorie reprimanded with a shocked gasp.

"Just kidding, Mother." Caroline tugged off her sweatband and snapped it at him, like a rubber band. "Rick knows that."

He knew she was a handful. A delicious handful.

"Oh, my." Marjorie glanced at her watch and rose, her feather-trimmed satin robes whispering around her. "Where has the time gone? I've got a hair appointment this morning, too. We'll talk later," she promised. Marjorie was gone in a whiff of perfume.

As soon as her mother had disappeared, Caroline set down her glass with a thud and exited through the French doors into the elaborately landscaped garden. There were no flowers this time of winter. She prowled the rows of rosebushes, her mood apparently as thorny as the branches she was studying.

"I didn't think you'd show up this morning," Caroline finally remarked.

She had a lot to learn about him, Rick thought. "I promised I would," Rick said.

"Look, I know you're having a grand time with all this."

"Better than I expected, even after I kissed you," he affirmed.

"But I have a business to run," Caroline continued.

He resisted the urge to take her into his arms and hold her close. "The past year hasn't been easy for you, has it?" he sympathized.

"If you're asking if I miss my father, the answer is yes. I miss him dearly." She took a tremulous breath and released it slowly. "He taught me everything I know about the business. We worked side by side for over eight years."

"So closely, in fact, it feels strange to be running the company without him?" Rick asked gently.

Caroline nodded and sat down on a stone bench, knees together, her hands on either side of her. "The business was his life. Now it's become mine." She paused. "He always said that it was a person's work that sustained them through good times and bad. And that's certainly been true in my case."

Rick had the feeling it wasn't that simple. Caroline wasn't working such long, hard hours simply because she missed her father. She'd been hurt. Otherwise, she wouldn't have so many defenses. She wouldn't look so moody and unapproachable whenever the subject of men and marriage came up. "Too much work and no play makes Caroline a dull girl," he teased.

"Maybe so," she countered lightly, "but I'd trade the dullness of security any day for the upheaval unpredictability brings."

Rick stretched out his legs in front of him, inspecting the polished toes of his favorite Western boots. "That's too bad, 'cause you've got an unpredictable streak a mile long in you."

Caroline bounced off the bench. "How would you know?" she called over her shoulder as she raced off down the meandering gravel path that snaked through the shrubs and flowers.

Rick caught up with her at the edge of a lagoon-shaped swimming pool. "I just do. Just like I know your life has been hard the past months because of more than just the power struggle within the company, or your grief. The fact of the matter is none of the major cosmetics firms have thrived without its founder. Max's successor is going to have to possess enough dazzling public cachet so that their persona can be inextricably intertwined with that of Maxwell Lord Cosmetics.''

Caroline's chin thrust out stubbornly. ''I can project that kind of cachet.''

''Then prove it to your board of directors,'' Rick urged.

''How?''

''Go public with your fight for the company presidency. Use your youth and beauty to make your image as public and strongly identified with the company as your father's was.''

Caroline shook her head, nixing his suggestion before she'd even had time to really absorb it. ''That's not my style.''

''Was it Max's in the beginning? Or did he grow into the persona?''

Caroline studied Rick coolly. In the morning sun, her hazel eyes looked more blue than green-gray. ''Why do you care so much about whether I make a go of it or not?'' she asked suspiciously. ''Why is this so important to you?''

Rick tore his eyes from the sunlight glinting on her hair. He studied the cabana with more than necessary care. ''I'd like to help you out, that's all.''

''Why?'' Caroline persisted heatedly.

Rick gave her a Cheshire cat grin, enjoying her unrelenting interest in him, then dared a look at her lips. They were as soft and imminently kissable as he remembered them. "Maybe I want your undying gratitude."

She shot him a feisty look. "Dream on."

Rick shrugged. "So I'll settle for the knowledge I tried and get some beautiful engagement photos of you instead."

Tossing her head, she planted both hands on her hips. "And if I refuse to cooperate?" Caroline challenged.

"With your mother looking on, waiting to prove you're trying to pull a fast one on her, I don't think you will."

Caroline said nothing for a long moment. Finally she sighed. "All right, you win. For the moment anyway. What kind of photos did you have in mind?"

"Something as glamorous as your position in the company."

She peered at him skeptically through thick dark brown lashes. "And that's it? That's all I have to do? Have my picture taken?"

He nodded. "Sounds simple, doesn't it?"

Caroline frowned. "Almost too simple."

"HOLD STILL, DARLING," Rick whispered, his warm breath caressing her ear.

"I would if you didn't have that blasted fan in my face."

Rick grinned, his hot glance skimming her from head to toe. "That blasted fan is doing wonderful things for your dress. Not to mention your hair."

"If I thought we could take an engagement photo without you in it ..." She wished for the millionth time that she had never agreed to wear this incredibly sexy dress Rick and her mother had picked out today while she was at work.

"I know, I know. You prefer to be in my arms. Don't worry, princess, that time will come," Rick teased.

"I prefer," Caroline corrected archly, "to be elsewhere."

In fact, given her druthers, she would have cleared up this mess at once, by calling his bluff last night when he'd announced to the world they were engaged. But she couldn't have done that without risking that Rick would decide to come clean and tell everyone that they didn't know one another at all. And if the board members found that out now, it would mean the end of her business career at Maxwell Lord. They'd fear she'd do business the way she ran her personal life. Chaotically.

That wasn't the case, of course. Caroline was extremely ethical and straightforward when it came to her work. She toiled diligently and wasted neither her time nor anyone else's. But a businesslike approach simply did not work with her mother. Which was why she was in this mess now, Caroline fumed. Because her mother always had to have her way. And what she wanted now more than anything was for Caroline to be married!

"Cute, isn't she?" Rick turned to the photographer, then amiably back to Caroline. "Did you know your eyes sparkle when you get mad?" he asked, deadpan. "Or that when you're impatient to be done with something, you get more color in your cheeks?"

Caroline jerked away from him. "Just. Don't. Touch. Me."

His sensual mouth gaped. He dropped the arm he'd been trying to lace around her waist and regarded her with shock. "You started it."

"I did not!"

"Oh, really. Just who grabbed who the other night?"

In a panic, Caroline touched her finger to his lips before he could say more. "Stop right there." She swallowed hard, praying Rick wouldn't blow the whistle on her now, especially since her mother was within earshot.

He grinned, mischief shimmering in his eyes. "Only if you distract me," he baited wickedly.

Her mother was watching the two of them in amusement. Caroline moaned softly, aware she had never felt more miserable in her life, "I am distracting you."

"Not enough." He waited until her chin jerked up. He lowered his mouth to hers and let it hover above hers a sensual millisecond before whispering naughtily, "Maybe you know a better way?"

Without warning, Caroline ached to kiss him, ached to know the sweet pressure of his lips on hers and the thrill that went with his kiss. Lightheaded from the images crowding her thoughts, she dragged in another deep breath and took a single step back from him. She angled her head up to better look into his eyes. The mirth she saw there gave her the strength she needed to put him in his place. "All I know is that I am losing what little of my patience is left." She wanted to be back at the office, working on her proposal for the new teen line.

Rick grinned unrepentently. "I wasn't aware you had any patience to begin with. Sock me—" he caught her hand as it curled into a fist "—and I guarantee Mario Shapello'll get a picture of that, too."

Caroline glared. She had been photographed countless times in her life, but she'd never been fussed over the way she'd been fussed over tonight. A hairdresser had done her hair, a makeup artist her face. The dress—a long figure-draping evening gown in indescribably delicate shades of indigo, lavender and midnight blue chiffon—had been fitted to her by the same wardrobe mistress that worked on all of her mother's movies. Rick was wearing a tuxedo, but no one was paying anywhere near the attention to him they were paying to her. Darkness had fallen hours ago. But their garden—which had been adorned with dozens and dozens of blooming flowers in all varieties—was lit up like it was midday. Why they couldn't have gone to some local studio and had the usual boring, posed engagement photo taken, Caroline didn't know.

"Must you make this ten times harder than it has to be?" she finally asked Rick.

"Hey. You're the one who's not cooperating, who stiffens up every time I take you in my arms."

Caroline closed her eyes and counted backward from one hundred. When she reached eighty, she said, "I can't help it. I'm tense."

"Want me to massage your cares away?"

Caroline's eyes flew open. Mario Shapello laughed. "You two," he chided, as he finished loading his camera with yet another roll of film.

"More fun than a barrelful of monkeys, aren't we?" Rick drawled.

"And then some," the photographer agreed. "Now hold her close, Rick. That's it. Your arm about her waist. Turn and look at him, Caroline. Gaze soulfully into his eyes."

Caroline turned and shot the photographer a mute, drop-dead look. He snapped that, too. She rolled her eyes and pushed away from Rick. He followed her through the garden, her chiffon dress floating around her like the softly falling evening mist.

"I'm sorry," he said quietly, catching up with her. He caught her wrist and tugged her close. "I'll behave."

Caroline gazed into his eyes. Dimly, she was aware that Mario had followed them and was still snapping away at them. She didn't care. She was no good at pretending, no good at living a lie, even if it did get her mother off her back. "You promise?" She couldn't take much more of this.

Rick nodded. "Cross my heart."

Their eyes held a moment longer.

"All right," Caroline said with a sigh, "I'll give it one more try."

"I KNEW YOU were lobbying hard for the presidency of Maxwell Lord, Caroline!" Hugh Bradford began harping before Caroline could so much as step off the elevator onto the executive floor.

"But don't you think this is taking it a little too far?"

Caroline shifted her stuffed briefcase to her other hand. "What are you talking about?"

Hugh's face was a blustery red. "The ads in the papers today," he supplied tightly.

Caroline cleared her mind of the dismal projections for their new men's line and her efforts to come up with a way to save it. "What ads? The ones promoting our new gift package at Foley's?"

Hugh scowled. "Don't pretend you don't know what I'm talking about." He shoved a folded newspaper at her. She stared down at a half page ad. It was obviously one of the photos Mario Shapello had taken in the garden. Rick had been completely cut out of the picture. It was a stunning photograph, rife with emotion. At the bottom of it was the caption in bold-faced print: The New Face Of Maxwell Lord Cosmetics. That was it; there were no other words or product logo on the page.

"That photo is in every major paper in the country. We've been getting calls all morning. The switchboard is jammed. Everyone wants to know who the new girl is, Caroline."

Caroline didn't know that she could look so ethereally beautiful, mysterious and yet romantically unapproachable. The girl in the photo was

Every Man's Dream, the girl he lusted after but couldn't have. And it wasn't really her. Was it?

Cy Rutledge joined them. He, too, had a newspaper in his hand. "Congratulations, Caroline." The head of advertising shook her hand warmly. "I was never sure how much you wanted the job until now. This photo of you proves you're willing to go all out to get it. Keep it up, and you've got my vote."

"Thanks, Cy."

Tony joined the group. "The ads were terrific, sis. You're one step ahead of me, for now."

"Tony, don't you dare do the same thing," Hugh warned.

"Don't worry." Tony grinned. "I'm no copycat. If and when I come up with something to top that—and I'll be honest with you, sis, I'm not sure I can at this point—it'll be as bold and imaginative as the workday is long around here." Tony patted Caroline on the shoulder and walked off with Cy. Before Hugh could speak again, several other members of the board joined them. Their reactions were universally positive.

"Well?" Hugh fumed, when he and Caroline were alone again. "Don't you have anything to say for yourself?"

Caroline gave Hugh a level look. "You've known all along how much I want the job," she said calmly. Rick knew, too. And bless his sneaky soul, he had gone all out to help. Better yet, he had placed the ads in such a way that she would get all the credit with the board. It was a brilliant move on his part.

Because Hugh was still looking at her accusingly, Caroline continued, "I'm not going to apologize for wanting to fill my father's shoes, Hugh."

Hugh stared at her. "Running that ad without consulting anyone on the board and replacing Max's image with your own was dirty pool, Caroline. I want you to know right now, as far as the company presidency goes, the gloves are off."

"I CAN'T DECIDE whether you're a devil or an angel," Caroline said when Rick entered her office later that day. "But I'm certain I want you out of my life." She watched him sink into a chair opposite her desk.

"Aw, Caroline, come on." Looking incongruous in her ultrafeminine office, which was decorated in the official Maxwell Lord colors of dusty rose and pearl gray, Rick kicked back in her chair and propped his feet up on one corner of her glass-topped desk. He was wearing a blue tweed jacket, with suede elbow patches. The first two buttons of his white oxford-cloth shirt were undone. His jeans were fashionably old and faded a medium blue.

They hugged his lower torso like a second skin. His boots, she'd seen before. Ditto the black felt cowboy hat.

"Don't be mad at me," Rick continued, tipping the brim of his hat back with one poke of his index finger. "The ads were for a good cause."

She was receiving accolades from every member of the board but Hugh, as well as from the public. And thanks to the hauntingly beautiful photograph of herself, she had also proven that she possessed the public cachet necessary to run the company. However, Rick had taken it upon himself to create a major new ad for *her* company.

Caroline stormed around her desk. "That's not for you to decide, Rick."

"The ads got you what you wanted, didn't they? Exposure on a national scale, not to mention a link with the company that's not ever going to go away?"

What she had gotten, Caroline thought, was a fake fiancé she didn't want and a life spinning out of control. "Listen to me, Rick. This is my family company—not yours. I call the shots."

"So I heard."

"Furthermore, your efforts to ingratiate yourself into my life are not working."

"Oh, I don't know about that." Rick crossed one ankle over the other and folded his hands temple-style over his lap. "Your mother seems to like me."

Caroline knocked his feet to the floor. "Her eight marriages are proof she has lousy taste in men."

"You may be right. How's *your* taste, Caroline?" Rick latched on to her wrist and vaulted her down onto his lap. "What do you like?" he asked softly, nuzzling her neck.

Caroline shoved with all her might at his chest. "I—"

She hadn't gained more than an inch when he clamped both his strong arms around her, anchoring one at her waist, the other the nape of her neck. Her gasp of moral outrage was stifled by the onslaught of his mouth on hers. Before she could do much more than register what was happening, he had tilted her head back and delivered a steamy kiss she felt all the way to her toes.

Face burning, senses reeling, she jerked her mouth from his, and stumbled to her feet. "Get this straight, Rick," she warned as she tugged at the hem of her skirt. "I am not your puppet on a string."

He lifted his serious green eyes to hers. "I wouldn't want you to be," he said softly. "I like you just the way you are. Sassy mouth. Fiery temper. Hard-as-nails ambition."

He hadn't described her in a way that was at all complimentary, and yet . . . he made her feel desirable. "Are you through?" Caroline asked coolly.

Rick rolled to his feet, sauntered toward her with easy, sensual grace. "Far from it, princess," he allowed with his honeyed Southern drawl. "But you're right. Maybe it is time for me to mosey along. As they say, I got my own fish to fry."

"Yeah, well, keep them out of my kitchen!" Caroline snapped. "And keep *yourself* out of my kitchen."

It was only later, after he'd moseyed on out of there, that she realized what a ridiculous thing that was to say.

HOURS LATER, Caroline walked into her River Oaks mansion to the smell of frying fish. Exhausted from a very long hard day, she went straight to the kitchen. Not surprisingly, her fiancé was standing in front of the stove, juggling a skillet and spatula with the ease of a man who'd cooked more than one dinner for himself. She stared at him stonily, not about to give an inch, even if the golden brown fish smelled delicious. "Where's my cook?" she asked calmly.

"I sent her home," Rick said, flipping a breaded fillet.

Caroline's stomach growled, reminding her she'd worked through lunch. "My mother?" Ten to one, Marjorie had played some part in this.

"She and Tony graciously agreed to eat out and give us time alone."

Caroline tore her eyes from his brawny forearms and pushed away the memory of how strong those forearms were when they were wrapped around her. So what if he made her feel more of a woman than she ever had in her life? So what if he was the master of sensual kisses? That didn't mean she had to give in to his lazy charm and boundless enthusiasm. "How do you do it?" Caroline asked.

"What?"

"Get your own way so much of the time."

Rick grinned, stuck his thumbs through the belt loops of his jeans and retained his arrogant stance before the stove. "Takes practice and a lot of gumption. Not that you're any novice yourself in that department, princess. Want a drink?"

"Why do I have the feeling you want something from me again?"

He held her eyes with his mesmerizing green gaze, making her feel all hot and bothered inside. "'Cause maybe I do."

His voice was soft and kind, yet something in her went cold. She despised being used, and the easy way he'd handled her thus far told her he was a master at getting what he wanted from women. "Like what? Money?" Caroline guessed in a flat, emotionless voice.

His gaze narrowed. Abandoning his duties at the stove, he moved closer, so they were almost touching. "I want something immeasurably more difficult to get and worth a hell of a lot more. Your time and attention."

"So?" Caroline lifted one shoulder in an elegant shrug. "You've got both." By default, she added silently. "Let's just get on with it, Rick." *Name your price.*

He studied her briefly, went back to turn his fish, and said, "You know how you feel at the end of every workday, not to mention every work week? Kind of tired and achy and drained?

Caroline nodded, feeling briefly reassured by the businesslike tone of his voice. "So?"

"What would make you feel better than anything in this world?"

"Knowing you're gone for good?" she asked lightly.

He grinned, enjoying her verbal jab as much as she had enjoyed delivering it. "Going to a full-body spa where you could be pampered and beautified from head to toe, just like at The Golden Door, all in a matter of hours," Rick corrected. "Only you wouldn't have to pay thousands of dollars or stay for a full week or even leave the city to do it."

"Unfortunately there is no place like that in Houston or anywhere else that I know of."

"Exactly. Don't you think there should be?"

Queen for a day. The idea appealed to the frazzled woman inside of her, just as she figured it would appeal to other women who felt just as overworked and underappreciated. Caroline sat down in a chair, kicked off her pumps and massaged her aching feet. She had business to attend to tonight. She had brought a briefcase full of work home with her. So they needed to wrap this up fast. "What are you getting at, Rick?"

Before he could answer, the back door slammed. Hugh rushed in. "Caroline. I'm glad I caught you."

Caroline slipped her shoes back on and stood up. "What are you doing here?"

Hugh shot an angry, distrustful look at Rick, then thrust a manila folder at Caroline. "I have something you might want to read."

Caroline glanced down at the sheaf of papers. "A private investigator's reports on Rick?"

Rick grabbed a fistful of Hugh's sweater and lifted him off the ground. "Where do you get off investigating me?"

Hugh shook free. Red-faced, he backed away from Rick, straightening the front of his sweater all the while. "He's an opportunist and a hustler, Caroline. It's all right there. Time after time, he has taken advantage of people, exploited their weaknesses and the weaknesses of the businesses they own and then profited—richly. He even started with a scam. He sued a car-wash owner for ruining the finish on his car, a beat-up old sports car. Then, when he won a judgment that put them out of business, he turned around, bought the joint, fixed it up and used the profits to buy another one in similar trouble . . . and so forth."

Caroline looked at Rick, her every gut instinct telling her there was some explanation. "What do you have to say about all this?"

"I say," Hugh interrupted, "if you continue with this engagement, Caroline, you'll be sorry."

Caroline continued to look at Rick. "Is it true? Did you really sue that car-wash owner?"

"Yes," Rick said. "And my '67 Mustang was not beat-up. It was a classic, restored to perfect condition, until those idiots got ahold of the finish, anyway."

"So you sued them, forced them out of business and then bought it?"

"It wasn't like that!"

But Caroline, knowing how quickly he'd barged into her life and made a mess of things, feared that her gut instincts were wrong. Hadn't she learned anything from the heartbreak of the past? she railed silently. When would she learn to stick to the facts as they presented themselves to her? Rick was an opportunist. He saw a way to profit. He made his move.

Her hands trembled as she scanned the rest of the reports on him. "Did you also invest in other car washes, dry cleaners, country-and-western beer halls?"

"Yes, I did."

"Did you also create the problems each of these businesses had that forced them into near ruin, and later forced them to sell to you?"

"What do you think?" Rick's eyes flashed angrily.

Caroline thrust the reports aside and ran her hands through her hair. "I don't know what to think. This is all pretty damning."

"Shame on you, princess, for falling victim to Hugh's plan to drive a wedge between us. You ought to know better than anyone things aren't always what they seem." His expression was as faintly mocking as his sardonic tone. Rick pivoted away from her and turned to Hugh. "If you think I'd ever harm so much as one hair on her head, you're stupider than I thought.''

"You're the fool," Hugh retorted, "if you think you can steal Caroline's business the way you've stolen everyone else's.''

Was that what Rick was after? Maxwell Lord Cosmetics? Caroline wondered, suddenly feeling a little sick. Was that why he'd snuck into her River Oaks home to meet her, romanced her, announced their engagement and run the ads—all so he could insinuate himself into not just her life but her company, as well?

Rick gave Hugh another searing look, rolled down his sleeves, fastened the buttons at his wrists, grabbed his sport coat and shrugged into it, all without saying a word.

"Rick, stay," Caroline said. "Talk to me." *Tell me this isn't so!*

"No thanks," Rick said tightly, pushing the words through a row of white even teeth. "I've got better things to do. I've never lied to you, Caroline. All I've tried to do is help you in any way I could. Think about that.''

He picked up his hat and shoved it onto his head. "Enjoy your dinner," Rick told Caroline softly. His eyes held hers a long time. "You can feed mine to Hugh. I've lost my appetite.''

Chapter Four

"I was wrong," Caroline said.

"Is that an apology?" Rick asked several days later. His voice was lazy, self-assured and faintly baiting.

"Yes." Caroline stood just inside his private office, very aware of the secretary on the other side of the closed door. She lifted her chin and angled her head back until she could see into his face. Aware her heart was pounding, she searched his eyes for any sign of forgiveness. "Will you accept it?"

"I don't know," he bit out. He swaggered closer, his steps long and lazy. In tight-fitting jeans and boots, a light blue oxford-cloth shirt worn open at the throat and a bone corduroy jacket, he looked rugged and male and as at ease in the lavish corporate setting of his Houston high rise as he had been in the kitchen and bedroom of her home. Just being near him again, Caroline felt her heart skip a beat, then chided herself for the hopelessly romantic reaction. She knew better than to let her feminine fantasies dictate her actions. Just because Rick looked and acted the conquering hero, did not mean he was the answer to her prayers, she told herself firmly.

His eyes had never left her face. "What made you change your mind?"

Caroline tried not to think what he was doing to her senses. "I took that list of businesses Hugh gave me and visited several of them," she said softly. "I was impressed by what I saw. I also talked to some of the employees. I learned you never put anyone out of a job unless they were performing below par and had no desire to improve. You have a very loyal group of employees working for you, Rick."

He nodded. "Yeah, I know. I'm fond of them, too. Is that all?"

"No."

"What, then?"

Caroline tried not to think about the way he never really told her what she wanted to know when she wanted to know it, or how fast her heart was beating right now or the edgy, incredibly alive way Rick made her feel whenever he was around. She swallowed around the knot of tension in her throat and told herself that wasn't joy she was feeling at seeing him again, so much as annoyance.

He hadn't called, hadn't popped in at her office or her home. Did that mean he had tired of the mess they'd both gotten themselves into? Was he tired of playing the part of her fiancé or just angry because she had wanted more proof that he was trustworthy. Worse, what if he backed out now? Then where would she be? In the soup, that's where, Caroline thought dismally.

"I wasn't sure I'd see you again," she said carefully.

He sauntered away from her. "We had a deal, remember?" he drawled in his heavily accented voice as he moved his trademark black Stetson aside. He propped his hips against the edge of the large oak desk. "No matter what you think of me, I couldn't leave you out to dry."

Caroline shoved both her hands into the pockets of her long, thigh-skimming blazer. "Is that what you think I did to you?"

His eyes glimmered with a cynicism that stung. "You're telling me it wasn't?"

She said nothing. She couldn't think of anything to say to that. Hugh's accusations had hit a nerve with her. She'd be lying if she said they hadn't. She'd been taken by a fortune hunter once. She was scared to death of it happening again.

Rick's eyes grew even grimmer. "That's what I thought. Well, fear not, princess, I won't do you any more harm."

Caroline heard the finality in his voice. "What do you mean?" she asked coolly.

"What do you think I mean?" He shoved back the edges of his jacket, revealing a slim hip and a washboard-flat stomach. "I'm letting you off the hook."

"Suppose I don't want to be off the hook?"

He leaned back and clamped his hands over the rock-hard solidness of his chest. "Too bad."

"Rick!" She rushed forward, aware she was behaving like a desperate woman, but no longer caring, so long as she got her way. "You can't walk out on me this way. What'll the board of directors think?"

"That's your problem."

"Damn you. You started this, too. You're just as culpable as I am here."

Rick cocked his head and gave her a thorough once-over. "This mean you're asking me to stay on as your suitor, princess?"

"Yes, Rick, I guess I am." She mocked his smart-mouthed drawl to a T.

Half his mobile mouth crooked up contemplatively. "But just to save your skin...."

She balled her hands in her pockets. "What other reason *could* there be?"

Rick shook his head in silent bemusement, gave her another long, assessing look, then stood and started for the door.

"Rick!" Caroline said. He stopped, but didn't turn around.

She started to touch his broad shoulders and force him to face her, then thought better of it and simply stepped around him, putting herself directly in his path. "What'll it take to square things with us again?"

He lifted a hand to his jaw and rubbed the angled contours with a slow deliberation she found extremely aggravating. "I don't know if it's possible to do that," he said finally, stepping toward her so that she was forced to back up. The sudden devil-may-care glint in his eyes was every bit as disturbing as his frank disappointment in her had been. "Your buddy Hugh is still out on a fact-finding mission, you know." He closed in on her deliberately, not stopping until only a scant two inches remained between them. He gazed down at her, like a hawk eyeing his prey.

"There isn't a friend or business associate of mine either he or that P.I. he's hired haven't called," Rick continued with exaggerated patience. "He even phoned my mother and half my sisters."

A private person herself, Caroline felt her heart go out to him. "I'm sorry," Caroline said. "He told me when he saw the ads he was going to start fighting dirty, but I had no idea you'd be the target."

"In that case, I suppose I deserve it. Since I placed the ads that demonstrated your potential as company spokesperson."

"But Hugh doesn't know that," Caroline pointed out. "No one does." Which made Hugh's actions all the more unscrupulous.

"Doesn't matter whether he knows or not. Hugh really upset my mother with all his talk of scams and money-oriented engagements. She doesn't want anyone thinking I'm a fortune hunter."

"What'd you tell your mother about us?"

Rick shrugged. "The truth. That'd I met a wonderful woman and she had another beau, Hugh Bradford, who was as jealous and suspicious of me as the day was long. And also determined to break us up."

Wasn't that the truth, Caroline thought. Which was ludicrous because she and Hugh had never been anywhere near engaged. "What'd your mother say?"

Rick grinned. "Just what I would've expected."

"Which is?"

"She told me to hang in there. Said if you were worth loving, you were worth fighting for."

The mention of the word *love* brought fire to Caroline's cheeks. "But we're not in love," Caroline corrected coolly.

"I know, and it's a shame, isn't it?" he said. As her eyes widened, he touched her face with the callused roughness of his palm, cupping her chin in his hand, scoring his thumb across her lower lip. "If we were . . ." His words trailed off slowly. She had the sharp suspicion he was about to kiss her. And the even sharper suspicion she'd be lost if he did.

She stepped away, admonishing bad-temperedly, "That's not why I'm here, Rick!"

He dropped his hand obediently and smiled, but not repentantly. "Sorry. You have a way of getting me sidetracked."

And vice versa, Caroline thought, flushing all the more. "What are we going to do?"

A hint of the old merriment sparkled in his eyes. He wrapped a hand about her waist. "Now?"

"About Hugh!" Caroline slipped out of his hold and danced away. "He's determined to discredit me. And he doesn't care how he does it. If he has a clue our engagement is a fake one, he'll waste no time in exposing us both."

And then they'd both lose, Rick thought. Unfortunately, even if Hugh didn't expose them, his own situation was far from assured. Caroline had reacted badly to even the accusation Rick might want something from her. When she found out what he'd been trying to tell her the other night, before Hugh barged into her kitchen and so rudely interrupted them, she was going to be just as unhappy.

"The best way to throw Hugh off our trail is to prove his suspicions about our engagement are wrong," he finally said.

Suddenly Caroline's heart was beating very quickly. She told herself it was the deception involved, not the thought of working closely and intimately with Rick, that had her head swimming. "How?"

Rick shrugged. "Well, first of all you'd have to at least act as if you trusted me, no matter what."

At his censuring look, Caroline realized she had hurt him. For all his foolishness, Rick was a man who wanted to be liked and taken seriously. "Easier said than done."

"Remember the other day, when we talked about the wisdom you got from your father? Well, my father had a saying, too. He said you could look into a man's eyes and see his whole heart and soul.

You've looked deeply into my eyes more than once, Caroline. What do you see?''

That was the problem, Caroline thought. She had one hell of a time trusting her feelings about men. "Your eyes are very nice, Rick. It's the way you charaded as a caterer and bulldozed your way into my home that still bothers me."

"Like you've never done anything off-the-wall to get what you want," he said dryly.

"That wasn't normal business procedure for me," Caroline said coolly.

"Well, me, either. I only twisted Marilu's arm to let me help out on the job as a last resort. I had tried to see you via the regular business route, but was told your calendar was crammed for months to come."

"No one told me you were trying to get in to see me!"

"So check it out with your administrative assistant now. She'll tell you I bugged her for weeks. All I wanted was the chance to talk to you. As it happens, I've got some interest in your area of expertise." Stepping closer, he pointed a lecturing finger at her nose. "You're the one who snagged me by the hand, dragged me up to your bedroom, offered to pay me extra and then ordered me to kiss you, princess! And all for the purpose of putting on a show for the rest of your family."

"Well, you don't know how much pressure I've been under." Caroline justified her actions hotly, as she paced back and forth, waving her arms in frustration. "Everyone doubting me at work and treating me like a kid who couldn't tie her own shoes without her daddy standing over her. And then, my mother, calling all the time, wanting to know when I'm going to get married. I *tried* being honest with her! Then I just made up a mystery man and said he was tall, dark and handsome, all the things I've ever dreamed of, and—"

"Whoa! Let me get this straight. You're saying I'm your dream man?"

Caroline blushed and ignored his question. "Anyway, that must've been when Mother got the idea to fly in and surprise me. Of course she picked the worst possible time. And of course she only gave me ten minutes' notice before she arrived on my doorstep."

"Ten minutes? That's all?" Rick asked, frowning.

"She called me on the way in from the airport," Caroline conceded dryly. "What was I to do? I dashed down the stairs, saw you and made that outrageous offer. I've regretted it ever since," she confessed hotly.

"I haven't," Rick admitted. "I enjoy spending time with you."

"You enjoy putting me on the hot seat," she pointed out archly. She wished he wouldn't look at her like that, like he knew every one of her foibles and enjoyed them all immensely.

"Almost as much as I'd enjoy having you in my arms."

Without warning, Caroline recalled the mesmerizing intensity of his kiss. "Would you be serious?" she demanded impatiently.

"I am being serious," Rick corrected as he slipped his fingers beneath her chin, drew her face up and studied her eyes. His gaze softened. "How come you never told me any of this before?"

"How come you never told me you'd tried to see me?"

He shrugged. "After we were officially engaged, it seemed beside the point. Anyway, the real question is how the board will see our engagement. I assume Hugh went to them with his private investigator reports."

"Yes, he did, but I set everyone straight. They all think—with the exception of Hugh, of course—that your strong ambition and ability to turn failing businesses into successful ones is something to be admired. As of now, my marriage to you is a strong asset to me."

"Good. I don't want your relationship with me to cost you anything, Caroline. I want you to gain from our association," he said firmly. "Not the other way around."

A few days ago, the company presidency was all that had mattered to Caroline. And though it was still important, she found she wanted Rick's respect, too. "So, you'll continue to help me?" she asked. "Even if Hugh continues to be difficult?"

Rick's expression softened. "I'm in this for the duration, come hell or high water or Hugh."

Heaven knew she wanted to trust him and believe he had no ulterior motives, but she just wasn't sure she should. He was right about one thing, though. They were in this for the duration. She couldn't back out. So right now she wouldn't think about what he'd meant when he hinted that someday he would like the two of them to do business together.

RICK JOINED HER in the testing lab adjacent to her office at eight o'clock the following evening. They were supposed to have dinner together, to pacify Caroline's mother. As usual, Caroline was having trouble breaking away from her work.

"I'll be ready to leave in a minute," Caroline told him in a clipped voice, her eyes focused on the clipboard in front of her, as she scribbled a few notes to herself. She was trying to decide which of the ten new products to offer as giveaways.

Rick studied the array of men's products set out on the lab's stainless-steel counters. "So what's all this?"

Caroline lifted her head. "Our new men's line."

"Oh." He frowned. His dark green eyes missing nothing, Rick looked around, his gaze finally fastening on a makeover booth. It contained a well-lit mirror, pump-operated beauty-salon-style chair and a sink. "That's why you're working such long hours these days, I guess. You're worried about launching it, aren't you?"

Caroline put down her clipboard. His comments were too close for comfort. "Why would I be worried?"

He shrugged. "You'd be a fool if you weren't, since your company has never had a successful men's line. Not that that's any surprise, of course."

The last thing she wanted to hear was Rick's discourse on her company's business failures. Nevertheless, her scalp prickled with uneasiness. "How do you know that?"

Rick looked her straight in the eye. "I always do my research," he said. "And I told you, I'm interested in possibly doing business with you someday. When are you going to launch it?"

Knowing that there was little to be gained from industrial espionage at this stage—the products were already patented and would be on the shelf and available for analysis anyway in two weeks—she relaxed and moved closer. "The actual launch is going to be timed for Valentine's Day. Our hopes for the line are very high. As per usual, we'll have a huge party formally introducing the product the day before it appears in the stores."

Their glances meshed. "You're worried about the launch, aren't you?"

Caroline sighed, knowing that although Rick might deride her for her ambition, he wouldn't demean her for worrying over quality and commercial success. "As you have probably already guessed, Rick, we've spent a lot of money developing the products. The board of directors is relying on Maxwell Lord for Men to bolster the sagging sales in the men's division. Unfortunately, if it's not an immediate success—and I'm talking banner sales in the first couple of days—we may have to just cut our losses and do away with the men's division altogether by the end of the fiscal year."

And she didn't want that for a myriad of reasons. She hated to give up on anything. She didn't want to let her father down. She didn't want to feel she had failed. And she didn't want that failure fresh in the board's mind when they voted on whether or not to make her the permanent president and CEO of Maxwell Lord.

Rick quirked a dissenting brow. His emotions mirrored how she felt. "That'd be a lot of money down the drain," he pointed out.

"Not to mention a lot of time and care and some very good products." Caroline sighed. "At any rate, advertising is key, so..." She picked up several posters the art department had sent her to peruse. "What do you think? We're putting together a free-gift-with-purchase for the launch. And we're also picking out the packaging."

For once, Rick didn't rush to give his opinion. "Don't you ever stop working?" he asked.

No, Caroline thought, she really didn't. And she liked it that way. Or at least she had until Rick had entered her life and shaken everything up. "No." She paused. "And maybe you shouldn't, either."

He lifted his head, his jade eyes flashing with interest. "Why is that, princess?" he drawled as if expecting a punch line.

She didn't disappoint him. "Maybe it'd keep you out of trouble."

He grinned roguishly and rubbed his jaw. "I doubt that. But maybe you should work less and play more."

It was tempting, but unpractical, Caroline knew. Who would watch over Hugh and Tony if she weren't around, riding herd on them both, keeping Hugh from being too conservative, Tony too reckless? No, the company would go to hell in a hand basket if she turned her back on it, even for a day. She knew that. As had her father before her. If their personal lives suffered because Maxwell Lord was a demanding mistress, then that was just the way it was.

"I can't," she said simply.

"Sure you can," Rick murmured persuasively. He stepped nearer. Caroline's heartbeat sped up to triple time.

Afraid she'd get lost in his mesmerizing gaze if she let their staring match continue, afraid she'd get lost in his kiss if he took her in his arms once again, Caroline turned her attention back to work once more.

She cleared her throat, effectively spoiling the sexy, thrill-a-minute mood she knew Rick was working his darnedest to create. "As I was saying, Rick," she said coolly. "Do any of these gift boxes appeal to you?"

He shrugged, making no effort to mask his disinterest in the boxes, and his continuing interest in her. "They all seem fine," he decreed without enthusiasm. "Masculine."

"But?" Caroline prodded.

"I don't think it's the packaging that is your problem." Rick looked at her directly and let out a slow breath. "It's where you're selling your men's line." He paused as if struggling with the need to spare her feelings, then went on bluntly, "Real men don't buy their shaving cream in department stores."

"Maxwell Lord products are far too expensive to be marketed in discount stores," she said defensively. "Furthermore, my father always said cutting prices meant cutting quality. Both are the kiss of death for people in our business."

"I agree with you," Rick said, "but that still isn't going to make men more inclined to shop for their shaving cream at Bloomingdale's. Not when they can buy Old Spice at the supermarket and be perfectly happy with it."

"They would if they tried our products."

"That's just it," Rick said with a mysteriously smug look, as if her argument somehow suited *his* purposes. "You'll never get them to try them sitting at the cosmetic counter in the front of the store."

Caroline planted her hands on her hips. Rick's resistance was typical. Here was her chance to delve deep. To do some hands-on market research with exactly the type of dashing, young, sexy men they wanted as their repeat customers. "You're telling me you wouldn't let me give you a facial?" Caroline asked in droll exasperation.

"Not in the front of the store, no," Rick said firmly. "I might run into someone I know, and even if I didn't..." Rick shook his head grimly, finding the whole idea unpalatable.

"In the department store's beauty salon, then?" Caroline pressed.

"Doubtful," he said in a terse, clipped tone. "Same reasons."

Caroline sighed. "In your local barbershop?"

"*Definitely* no. Though I don't get my hair cut in a barbershop, I go to a unisex salon."

"Would you have it done there?"

Rick thought about that for all of one minute. "And be seen with some stupid mask on my face by members of the opposite sex? Not great for the old male ego, you know?"

Caroline knew. Boy, did she know. "What about here, then? What about now—in my testing lab?"

Rick grinned, a little put off by her persistence. "We're supposed to go to dinner."

"So dinner can wait."

"Our reservations—"

"We'll have a hamburger at McDonald's later, okay? I don't care about what we eat. I'm interested in my research here. So how about that facial?"

"You really want to do that?" he asked incredulously. "Now?"

"Yes, Rick, I do." If she could convert Rick, she could convert anyone.

He studied her a moment longer. "Sure." He was already shrugging off his corduroy sport coat and hanging it over the far end of the counter. "Why not?"

"Okay. Sit here." Caroline patted a swivel chair, took off her designer blazer and shrugged on a pristine white lab coat.

Rick paused in the act of assuming a seat and glanced at her with comical dubiousness. "This isn't going to hurt, is it?"

"Trust me." Caroline clamped a hand on his muscular shoulder and pushed him the rest of the way down into the chair. Once he was situated comfortably, his long legs stretched out in front of him, Caroline pumped up the chair, until he was at the right height, then tipped him back to a reclining position. "This is going to make you feel great. We're going to start with a clay mask."

He caught her hand. "You're sure you know what you're doing, now?" he teased softly. "I don't want to end up with green or purple skin."

"You think I'd do that to you?"

"Yep."

He was right. She had been tempted, a number of times. "Relax," Caroline said, planting a reassuring hand on the firm width of his shoulder once again. "I'm trying to sell you on our products, not scare you off for good."

"You really enjoy this, don't you?"

"Sure. Selling cosmetics and grooming products is generally a very rewarding experience." She could see Rick was unconvinced.

"Kind of like selling snake oil, huh?" he teased.

"Like selling hope," Caroline corrected firmly as she whipped out a cape and spread it over his chest and shoulders. "Hope that a person can be more beautiful."

Rick squinted at her, trying to read her mind. "Clearly you have your doubts about me," he guessed.

Glad he was so far off the track, she said, "Nonsense. Our products can make anyone look better."

He grinned. "Even scoundrels?"

She raised a brow. "Even scoundrels. Now, just sit back and relax...." She worked on clear plastic gloves, then began to smooth a creamy mask over his face. Although Caroline had given facials scores of times—her father had insisted she learn the business from the ground up—this was different somehow. Maybe because she was so acutely aware of every inch of Rick she was touching: the you-can-get-along-with-me-or-go-to-hell lines of his jaw, the high masculine cheekbones, straight nose and oh-so-sexy mouth.

Aware of the tingling that had started in her chest and was working its way down into her tummy, she searched for something efficient and businesslike to say to him and instead blurted out the first inane sales-speak that came to mind. "Doesn't this feel good?"

Rick grinned. "Not as good as your hands, princess." He reached for her waist and began to reel her in.

Her heart hammering in her chest, her mouth dry, Caroline held on to her surface composure by a thread and elbowed his hands aside. "I'll tell you what I tell all the men I test our products on," she said sternly.

"And that is?"

"Behave."

Rick stretched out his lanky frame, put his clasped hands behind his head and crossed his legs at his ankles. "I was afraid you'd say that," he drawled. "What's next?"

"We wait five minutes." Caroline felt his eyes skimming along the backs of her legs as she moved about the room, gathering ingredients and utensils.

"Then what?"

"I wet a washcloth and gently rinse the mask off," Caroline told him. She returned to his side and went to work. Rick shut his eyes. Watching him sprawl so docilely in the chair, looking so content to have her hands upon him, made her wonder what it would be like to have him in her bed. Not as part of the ruse she'd hastily cooked up, but for real. Would he be this malleable then? Or would he be as insatiable and demanding a lover as his kisses implied?

"Next," Caroline told him, a little hoarsely, "I'm going to use an almond scrub."

"What's it do?" Rick asked.

"It removes the dead skin cells," Caroline said calmly, though inwardly she was a jangle of sensually ravaged nerves and unexpectedly lustful thoughts. She forced her mind back to the business at hand once again.

She gently rinsed off the scrub and applied astringent. Then she applied moisturizer over his face with a soft cotton pad. Finished, she straightened, removed his cape, put it aside. "Now, doesn't your skin feel great?"

Rick sat up. He looked surprised as he touched his hand to his face. "Well, what do you know," he murmured in amazement. "It does."

Telling herself how good Rick looked was of no professional interest to her, she leaned down to apply lip balm to his mouth with quick expert strokes and saw the straight white edges of his teeth and the pink hint of his tongue. Remembering how expertly he'd kissed her and how thoroughly she had been seduced into kissing him back, her heart raced. Her knees wobbled. Albeit a little dizzily, she straightened, faced him purposefully and announced with as much professional satisfaction as she could muster, "Ta da! You're done."

"Not quite." Rick said. The next thing Caroline knew, she was sprawled across his lap. "I won't be *done*," he continued, "until I've done *this*."

His mouth covered hers, and in that moment, everything stopped. The world narrowed to just the two of them. She knew she should fight him. The office was no place to have a liaison, but as his mouth gently contoured to hers—sipping, caressing, laving—all thoughts of resistance fled. She had waited a lifetime to be kissed like this. She had waited a lifetime to feel like this. And she'd be damned if she could stop it.

"Rick—" she murmured as he touched his tongue to her lips.

"I know, princess," he said, as his hand moved up to cup her breast. "I want you, too. So much."

Want. Not love. Want. The words sounding like
an alarm in her brain, Caroline pried his hand from
her breast, pressed both hands to his chest and
pushed. He withdrew his mouth from hers reluctantly, looking as dazed and lovestruck as she felt.
But he wasn't in love with her, Caroline reminded
herself firmly. He wasn't even pretending to be.

"Rick, no," she said breathlessly, as the heat of
her shame filled her face. She'd been acting like a
hormone-driven teenager, with no common sense!
"We—we can't."

"Why not?" he asked softly, his expression
yearning and tender, his eyes glowing with a determined, sensual light. "Everyone else has gone
home for the day. There's no one else in the building but us—"

It would take very little effort on his part to seduce her into picking up where they'd just left off.
Her physical reaction to him was that unexpected
and that intense. Caroline pushed away from him
deliberately. "We just can't, all right!"

She didn't even know what he wanted from her
yet, save her joint participation in some business
venture....

She stood on shaking legs and drew her white lab
coat around her like a cloak, glad for the cover it

afforded her breasts, which were still taut with arousal. "I think you'd better go."

Rick studied her in silence. Finally he picked up his corduroy jacket and shrugged it on. "Sorry, princess," he said gruffly. "We have to see your mother."

Chapter Five

"An engagement party?" Caroline asked.

"How else would you suggest we announce your upcoming marriage?" Marjorie returned. She sat perched on the satin settee in the formal living room of Caroline's River Oaks home, the full skirt of her indigo silk dress spread about her like a royal cloak.

Next to her glamorously attired mother, Caroline usually felt about as interesting as yesterday's newspaper. Yet tonight, the way Rick kept looking at her, Caroline had never felt more beautiful.

Wasn't it enough he induced her to confide in him her most intimate thoughts? That she'd kissed him with an appalling lack of restraint? Did he have to remind her with every possessive dark green glance how much more pleasure they could have if she'd only let things progress a little further into her bed?

"Your mother's right, Caroline," Rick was saying. "We should do this the old-fashioned way."

Caroline didn't want to think about what else he wanted to do the old-fashioned way. His steamy kiss back at the lab had been proof enough of his intentions. Because he wasn't sure she'd go for his business proposition he intended to seduce her. She was just as determined not to let him.

Marjorie said, "I've already notified the press. I've got reporters coming from the *Chronicle*—"

Caroline groaned, her misery complete. She wished she could go upstairs, take off her suit, sink into a steamy bubble bath and not think about this conspiracy that threatened to overtake her life. "Why not just invite 'Geraldo'?" Unfortunately, her thinly veiled sarcasm was lost on her publicity-loving mother.

"Well, darling," Marjorie said, beaming, "now that you mention it..."

"Mother!" Caroline interjected, truly horrified. "You didn't!"

"No, honey, I didn't," Marjorie was quick to reassure her. "But frankly, it wouldn't surprise me if a camera crew from 'Entertainment Tonight' showed up. After all, you are my only daughter and the fact you're getting married *is* news."

"So when is this party?" Rick slid his arm about Caroline's waist. Wary of making her mother any more suspicious than she already was, Caroline reluctantly leaned into Rick's solid male warmth.

"It's tomorrow evening," Marjorie said.

"Tomorrow evening!" Rick and Caroline echoed in unison.

"Isn't that a little fast?" Caroline asked.

"Not if you know the right people. Besides, my social secretary and assistant have flown out to help with the details. I put them both up in a hotel." With that, her mother stood, then headed toward the phone that had begun to ring in the next room.

Great, Caroline thought, *just great.* What have I done to deserve this except keep to the straight and narrow path?

"Don't look so distressed, Caroline. All you have to do is find a dress and show up," Rick said.

"I do not," she said, suddenly sick of the whole mess. "I'm not going."

"Then neither am I," Rick said.

"DID YOU GET MR. CASSIDY on the line yet?" Caroline asked her secretary, Sue Ellen, late the following afternoon. Now, Caroline was sorry for her burst of temper the previous evening. And she was half-afraid Rick wasn't going to show up at the party.

"Sorry, Ms. Lord," Sue Ellen replied, handing Caroline a stack of phone messages. "His service says he is still out."

"Out where?"

Sue Ellen glanced at the steno pad in her hand. "At a building he's remodeling over on Westheimer."

"Do you have the exact address?"

The young woman smiled. "I'm way ahead of you."

"Thanks," Caroline said, after she'd written it down.

"Ms. Lord?" Sue Ellen paused in the doorway. "About your engagement—congratulations."

"Thank you." Caroline smiled. She only wished she felt as lucky as everyone seemed to think she was. You'd think, by the way everyone was acting, that a woman needed to get married to feel complete. But she knew that wasn't true. She was perfectly happy. She didn't need a man or marriage. And she didn't need Rick.

Just because he was the sexiest man she had ever come in contact with and just because he made her go all weak in the knees when he kissed her was no reason for her to lose her head. She was a smart woman. Smart enough to stay in control.

"What about the ads for the new men's line?" Sue Ellen asked, trotting after Caroline to the elevator. "The agency sent some more over for you to look at this morning. They're anxious to have a reaction. Not just from Cy, but you."

"I'll study them late tonight and talk to Cy first thing tomorrow."

"Tony called," Sue Ellen continued efficiently. "He said he has to have a decision about what products are going to be in the giveaway for Maxwell Lord for Men, so he'll know how much of what and when to ship."

"I'm still waiting for Hugh's report," Caroline said, irritated to find the report delayed yet again. As head of marketing, Hugh's input was vital, even if he and Caroline were no longer getting along.

"Tony'll be unhappy about the delay," Sue Ellen warned. "He said the shipping orders should've been entered in the system yesterday."

"I know." Caroline frowned, very much aware of the way the race for the company presidency was dividing them all. Tony, Hugh and she were no longer working as a well-rehearsed team, but as three separate entities, eager to protect and promote their own interests. "But we've shipped products at the last minute before, with no problem. I'm sure we can do it again."

CAROLINE FOLLOWED the sound of the hammering. Rick was standing in the middle of what appeared to be a giant laundry room, nailing shelves to the wall. In worn jeans and a denim work shirt, he had never looked more masculine or appealing.

"You're a hard man to track down," she said, stepping around a sawhorse and over a bucket of nails.

Rick glanced at her over his shoulder. "I figured if you wanted to see me bad enough you'd find me."

"Why didn't you return my phone calls today?"

He went back to hammering steadily. "Used to having men jump through hoops, are you, Caroline?"

"No." Caroline blushed, since it was true.

"Yeah, right," Rick drawled. He sent her a glance that let her know *he* didn't intend to jump through any hoops. Seeming more enamored of his task than of her, he continued in a curt, disinterested tone, "So. What couldn't wait until tonight?"

Relief warred with hope. "That means you're coming to the engagement party?"

"Actually," he said, parroting her prim tone, "I haven't decided yet."

I knew I shouldn't have said I wasn't going, Caroline thought. But considering his kiss . . . and that look he'd had in his eyes . . . like he'd like to do it all over again, what choice had she had? "What do you mean you haven't decided?" she squeaked.

He shrugged and pivoted slowly to face her. He lounged back against the unshelved wall to their left, one booted foot across the other, his body at a slant. "It's not as if we've talked about it," he said, putting his hammer on the shelf beside him. "You went to bed with a headache so fast last night. Remember?"

Caroline began to rub at her temples again as the tension within her built. She wasn't used to lying, and the deception they had whimsically concocted was really giving her conscience a workout. "I had a headache!" she pointed out temperamentally.

"Yeah." Half his mouth crooked up. Delicious lights sparkled in his eyes.

Caroline thrust out a pouty lower lip and planted both her hands on her trim hips.

Rick's gaze trailed lazily over her long navy blazer and short pleated skirt. "You're the one with all the bright ideas," he said as his gaze drifted lower to her dark blue stockings and matching navy pumps. "I've just been going along with them to save your skin." His gaze detoured to the single strand of long pearls looped around her neck, moved across the white satin camisole blouse. Caroline waited impatiently for his slow moving perusal to get past her breasts to her face. It was a long, sensually laced wait.

"If you want me to feel guilty about lying at this point, considering all that's at stake, you've got a long wait," she advised coolly, not about to let him get the upper hand.

His grin widened. "I like the fire in your eyes when you're ticked off at me."

Caroline flushed again. If she didn't need him so much, she'd tell him where to go. But she did need him. Years of dealing with her overbearing movie-star mother had taught Caroline the only way to survive was to at least pretend to appease her mother. And that, Caroline reassured herself firmly, was all she was doing.

She would break her engagement with Rick soon enough. She would tell her mother she and Rick weren't suited for one another, which was the truth. And that would be that. Rick would be on his way. She would be on hers. End of love story. Only her mother would be disappointed, Caroline reassured herself.

In the meantime, however, she had to buy herself some more time, and unfortunately, that did require Rick's help. Assuming a don't-mess-with-me-fella pose, she crossed her arms. "Are you coming to the party or not?"

He sauntered to her side. "Do you *want* me to come?"

Caroline sucked in her breath at the unexpected gentleness of his voice and stepped back, out of reach. "It would be nice, yes," she retorted primly.

"What do I get if I help you out?"

"My gratitude?" Caroline asked hopefully.

He shook his head slowly, his eyes never leaving her face. "Not good enough."

Caroline blushed, able to read his thoughts as easily as any book. "I am not offering you anything else."

His eyes sparkled as heat climbed from her neck into her face. "Like what?" he asked with choir-boy innocence.

"You know what!" she said.

He lifted his hands helplessly. "No, I don't."

The hell he didn't, she thought. "I am not going to go to bed with you."

Rick's sensual lips parted in surprise. "Did I ask you to go to bed with me?" he asked, feigning shock.

"No," Caroline retorted drolly, beginning to pace the newly painted-and-tiled room, "but you look at me like you would." *And you kiss like it, too.*

"I suppose that would be nice," he finally said.

He reached for her and she snatched her hand away from his. Too late—he'd already captured her palm and pressed it to his chest, over the region of his heart. "Feel how my heart beats for you, Caroline." he said softly, stepping so close that their bodies were almost touching. "It pounds like that every time you get near me," he murmured.

So did hers. The moment drew out as she gazed into his eyes. She drew her hand away and swallowed hard around the tension gathering in her throat. "Sex is not going to enter into our relationship."

Rick shrugged. "If you say so." He looked confident otherwise.

Caroline started to run a hand through her hair nervously, then recalled she had restrained the thick wavy length of it in a prim bow at the nape of her neck, as she did almost every business day. She settled with just adjusting her pearl drop earring. "So what do you want, in exchange for helping me out tonight, if not more money?"

"Hmm." Rick rubbed at his clean-shaven jaw. Eyes glimmering with barely checked humor, he teased, "That's a hard one, princess. Since I can't take you to bed—"

"Trust me," Caroline interrupted in her most nononsense voice, knowing she couldn't risk another of his kisses for fear of what would happen, "you can't."

"Then I guess I'll have to settle for something else. Something meaningful.... I've got it."

Here it comes, Caroline thought. The business pitch she didn't want to hear, followed by blackmail, or even worse, a demand for hush money.

Rick snapped his fingers. "How about a home-cooked meal?"

"You're kidding. Aren't you?"

"What's the matter?" he taunted boldly. His hands caressed the width of her shoulders. "Can't cook?"

Her pulse racing, she stepped out of the light embrace. "Of course I can cook," Caroline retorted, sucking in several shallow breaths. Darn Rick for putting her off balance once again by moving the conversation from business into the personal arena.

"So what's the problem?"

You, she thought. You're the problem. "I am not the type of woman who cooks and cleans for her man," she announced.

Rick's gaze fastened on her mouth. "I'm your man?"

Caroline blew out an exasperated breath. She wished he would stop looking at her that way, like she looked good enough to eat. "You know what I mean,'' she retorted temperamentally, resisting the urge to fan herself. Was it hot in here or what? He certainly looked cool enough, but she was on fire.

"Yeah, I guess I do. And I know you're not exactly the housewife type, but a meal's what I want anyway," he said.

"Why?" Caroline asked, exasperated.

"Cooking is more intimate than money." Rick unbuckled the tool belt that hung around his lean hips and set it aside. "More meaningful. And for you—" he looked her straight in the eye "—I'd wager it's a lot harder to give."

How right he was about that! Caroline hadn't cooked for a man since the days when she'd been married, and she didn't intend to start again, either. At least not with any real aim to please. "Fine," she said shortly. "I'll cook you a dinner," she promised, "and have it delivered—"

"Whoa!" He silenced her with a finger to her lips. "I don't want you just delivering a basket of home-baked goodies to my place."

"Why?" she asked dryly. "Would it remind you too much of Red Riding Hood visiting the wolf?"

"Maybe. I can see myself in bed. I can't see myself in your granny's clothes."

Caroline couldn't see that, either. She could easily envision him in bed, however, gloriously naked, gloriously sexy.... She had to stop this. The sheer lustfulness of her thoughts was not helping.

Rick continued his list of demands. "I want to see you make the dinner. And I want to see you make it at my place."

Caroline rolled her eyes. "For what possible purpose?"

"For one thing, Marjorie and Tony won't be there."

He had a point in wanting the rest of her family gone. It was always sticky when they were around. More complicated somehow. And yet helpful, too, because she could use their presence as a shield against Rick's desire for her, and hers for him. "I can't convince you to take anything else as payment?" she propositioned sweetly. "Like a vacation in the Bahamas or...or maybe we can talk business." *And you can pitch that idea to me that I really don't want to hear.*

"Nope," Rick interjected firmly. "A home-cooked meal at my place or nothing."

"All right. You win. But in exchange I want you on your best behavior tonight at the party," Caroline specified. "No unnecessary kisses. No volunteering any more information than exactly necessary."

Rick nodded, agreeing to her demands without quarrel, then asked simply, "What do I wear?"

"Just something nice. A suit and tie. Mother told me this morning it's going to be semiformal."

"Which suit?"

"I don't know!" Caroline said. "You choose."

"That's going to be awfully hard for me to do, princess. After all, what do I know about these high-society parties?"

Her pulse racing, Caroline scowled at him. "You really have to be difficult, don't you?"

Their gazes meshed for one long breath-stealing moment. He smiled back at her. "It's part of my charm."

I won't fall for this guy. I won't. I won't. I won't. I don't care how alive he makes me feel. "Or lack of it," she corrected.

Rick merely continued to look at her in a way that made her feel very nervous. "Is that a yes— you'll help me find something to wear?"

She emitted a beleaguered sigh and told herself she might as well do the most expedient thing. "It'll be faster than arguing with you all day."

"THIS IS NICE, RICK."

Rick followed Caroline Lord into his Memorial Drive town house. "You sound surprised," he remarked with a smile as she strolled across the polished oak floor to the long white sofas that formed a conversation pit in front of a redbrick fireplace.

Caroline glanced approvingly at the heavy wooden beams adorning the cathedral ceiling, then strode past a glass-topped coffee table to the floor-to-ceiling windows that looked out on his lavishly landscaped patio. "I am."

Rick took his time getting to her side.

He wasn't used to putting his ambition on hold, even for a minute. And yet, he didn't want to hurt her. He didn't want her jumping to wrong conclusions and thinking he was only here because of what she could give him in a business sense. He'd have to get to know her a little more, try and stay out of her bed—though he didn't know if that was possible considering how hot their kisses had been—and hope for the best.

Once at her side, he braced a shoulder against the window and tipped his head down at her. "Where'd you think I'd live?" he teased. "Some dirty little hovel?"

Caroline tossed her head imperiously. Color swept into her angelically high cheeks. She pursed her soft, bow-shaped lips together. "Frankly, I hadn't given it much thought," she retorted airily.

Rick just bet she hadn't. She probably tried to think about him as little as possible. He knew he was trying his darnedest not to obsess about her. He knew he never should've backed her into a corner the way he had. He could have helped her out of the mess she'd gotten into with Marjorie, instead of backing her farther into the woman's web. But something about her willfulness had urged him on, dared him to give her the hardest time possible and teach her a thing or two about men.

"I don't suppose you keep your suits in the hall closet?"

"Not a chance, sweetheart. My bedroom closet's this way." He started to take her arm. She resisted it. He led the way.

Caroline looked at the skylight over his king-size bed but didn't say a word. He led her to the spacious walk-in closet with the U-shaped clothing racks.

"So which one?" he asked in a bored tone, not really caring what he wore to this soiree. But apparently she did, he thought, as he watched Caroline thumb single-mindedly through the long rack of his suits. "The pin-striped suit is out. Too bankerish."

"What about this one?" Rick fingered the one nearest him.

"Glen plaid is nice..."

"But?" Rick prompted as he watched Caroline walk slowly down the line. She looked slim and neat and pulled together in a proper sort of way. Even her hair, usually a riot of thick bittersweet choco-

late curls, was pulled back tightly in a ribbon bar-
rette at the nape of her slender neck.

"The plaid'll clash with my suit." At the end of
the rack, she rested an elbow on the clothes rod and
turned to look at him.

"Which is...?" Rick stepped close enough
to smell the wildflowers-in-a-sunny-meadow-fra-
grance of her perfume.

Her soft mouth lifted in a pleased smile. "Dusty
rose and pearl gray."

He paused. He knew she was a workaholic. That
had been obvious from the start. He didn't know
she carried her devotion to her family's business to
that extreme. "You're kidding, aren't you?"

She blinked, surprised at the question. "No."

He stared at her in disbelief. "You're wearing a
suit to our engagement party in Maxwell Lord colors?"

Caroline's chin took on a defiant tilt. "You're
the one who told me I needed to be inextricably
linked with Maxwell Lord," she said.

"In business," Rick corrected, irked she'd mis-
construed his words. "The party is personal."

"Not in my mind."

"Don't worry, once you win the company presidency, I'll be out like a shot," he said, his voice
laced with irony.

Caroline gave him a censuring look. "We agreed, Rick."

"Yeah, well, maybe I shouldn't have," he growled. Hadn't he realized from the start this princess only cared about one thing—her own career? He knew better than to get involved with women who were blinded by their own ambition, and yet here he was, sucked into her web just the same.

Caroline elbowed her way past him and stalked into the center of his bedroom. "What do you mean?" She gave him a cool, amused look, one that told him there was no softness inside. He knew better.

"I mean maybe it's time someone taught you the difference between business and pleasure," Rick drawled.

The next thing Caroline knew she'd been bent backward from the waist. Ignoring her muffled gasp of protest, he took her lips with the passion she'd ached to know again. For the first time in her life, she was with a man who wouldn't hesitate to give her the complete uncompromising physicality she had always craved. She reveled in it. Reveled in the hard, insistent demand of his mouth over hers and the urgent sweep of his tongue.

Her mouth was hot and wonderful beneath his. She tasted of mint. And woman. Slipping his fin-

gers through her hair, Rick did what he'd wanted to
from the moment he'd seen her that afternoon. He
loosened the clasp at the nape of her neck and let
his fingers tunnel through the rich silk of her hair.
She moaned and sagged against him, the bulk of
her weight resting against his bent knee. He could
feel her trembling, just as he could see the longing
in her eyes. Caroline might put up walls around her
heart; she wanted nothing more than for someone
to tear them down.

"Rick—" she whispered in a stunned voice,
when she could breathe.

Aware he hadn't begun to have his fill of her, his
lips moved over the softness of her neck. She
melted against him, her hand curling around his
shoulders. And yet there was so much more to be
conquered. Rick had always wanted a mysterious
woman. A woman who was strong but soft, stubborn but generous. He knew she'd been hurt badly
in the past; that was obvious from her resistance to
him. But he'd been hurt, too. It didn't mean they
had to spend the rest of their lives alone. Or even
one more day.

"Damn, but you're sweet and feminine all over,"
he murmured, sweeping her up into his arms and
carrying her to his bed.

She sucked in a quick breath, looking both pan-
icked and enthralled. "Rick!"

He deposited her in the center of the bed, and followed her down onto the satin spread. "What?" He gave her a long steady look.

"I—you—" she sputtered, but she made no move to get up. They were sprawled length to length in the middle of his bed.

Caroline knew she should get up, move away, do something, but she couldn't. It wasn't fear that held her spellbound. It was the promise she saw in his eyes. The tenderness.

"Kiss me again, Caroline," he pleaded softly, slipping a hand beneath her chin. His mouth lowered slowly, deliberately. "Just once."

Caroline meant to resist him, she swore she did, but there was just something about the way his lips moved on hers, so provocatively and surely, that totally sapped her will. There was just something about the feeling of his warm, hard body aligned with hers that made resisting him impossible. He was just so strong. So determined, and yet so giving. Lying there in the center of his bed, with the weight of his body draped over hers, their bodies in contact in all the right places, she had never felt so much a woman nor been as aware of any man.

As the kiss continued, he separated her legs with his knees and slid between them. Her skirt rode up. He pushed it even higher, then ran his palms down the sleek bare insides of her thighs. A shudder ran through him, then her. "Garters," he murmured, unsnapping first one, then another. "Why, Caroline, who would've thought..."

Caroline smiled at his pleasure and groaned low in her throat. He didn't know that the garters were new, that she'd had them forever—had bought them in a moment of whimsy—but had never worn them until this very day. She'd never had anyone in her life she wanted to wear them for. "Rick—"

"I know, princess, I'm getting there. But first, I've got to see—oh, Caroline..." He sucked in a shallow breath as he unbuttoned her blouse and unfastened her bra, baring her rosy nipples and creamy breasts to view. "You're beautiful."

With him looking at her that way, half in awe, she felt beautiful. Inside and out. He caressed her breasts, then bent and laved the raised nipples with his tongue, until they were tight and achy. "Rick," she moaned again, as a hunger unlike any she had ever known built within her. He was making her want, making her need....

"More?" he asked softly.

Yes, she thought, oh yes.

Not waiting for her reply, he slid his fingers inside the elastic of her bikini panties. Her hips rose instinctively to meet him as he touched and rubbed and stroked. Dizziness swept through her in waves. The hot, melting feeling in her stomach grew. And still their kisses continued, as hot and rapacious and searching as his touch.

It had never been like this for her, not even with Armand.... And even though she knew it was wrong, crazy even...the woman in her was tired of fighting. She needed to be loved in this fundamental way. It had been so long since anyone had held her. And no one had ever loved her so fiercely and possessively. Needing to touch him, her hands moved to his shirt, eagerly dispensing with the buttons.

"That's it," he murmured against her open mouth. "Touch me, too." He clasped one of her hands. "Here." He held it flat so she could feel his thundering heart, then slid it lower, across the rock-hard muscles of his stomach to the cold metal of his belt. "And here." He slid it lower, over the smooth, hard ridge in his jeans.

She no longer needed to protest. All she needed was now. This moment. This man. And the way he made her feel.

Trembling, Caroline complied with his wishes. She did what she had never done before and took the lead. To aide her, he slid onto his side. She unbuckled his belt, sucked in a shallow breath and drew down the zipper. Like hers, his skin was so hot, it sizzled to the touch. She marveled at the smooth, velvety hardness and the depth of his need. A need she had created and could ease.

Groaning in ecstasy, he rolled onto his back and took her with him. His hand cupped the back of her neck, and he brought her mouth down to his once again, his lips covering hers in a hunger and desperation she not only understood but felt, too. Life wasn't simple. Neither was this. Life didn't come without consequences. Neither would this. And yet, some pleasures were worth suffering for....

He whisked off her panties, and impatiently pushed down his jeans. The touch of flesh on flesh was electric. She moaned soft and low in her throat.

"Oh, Rick," she urged, bringing him closer. She was desperate to feel all of him, deep inside her.

"Now?" Rick asked, his voice ragged.

"Yes," she whispered. She wanted to feel everything. Every tremble. Every gasp. She clasped the smooth, warm muscles of his back and dug her fingers in. "Oh, yes."

His arms still around her, his body trembling with the effort it took to contain his own pressing need, Rick gently shifted his weight and rolled so that she was beneath him once again.

Caroline found herself on her back, with one knee raised, cupping the outside of his hip. She moaned again as their bodies aligned, flesh to flesh, and gazed up at him with eyes that were glazed with passion. This was incredible. He was incredible. He knew just where and how and when to touch. She wanted their lovemaking to last forever.

He slid inside her, watching her face as he entered her. He slid one arm beneath her hips and arched her lower body against him. "That's it," he whispered, deepening his penetration even more, "take all of me, Caroline, all of me."

He began to thrust inside her, slowly at first, then with building passion. Awash in sensation, Caroline closed her eyes. She was able to hear the soft, whimpering sounds in the back of her throat, unable to believe she was making them. Moaning the depth of his own satisfaction, Rick kissed her again, his body taking up the same timeless rhythm as his tongue. So this is what it should be like, Caroline thought.

And then all was lost in a blazing explosion of heat.

CAROLINE'S BREATH HAD barely slowed when she rolled away from Rick and cradled her head in her hands. Trembling and flushed, she struggled to simultaneously rearrange her clothing and sit up on the edge of the bed. "I can't believe I just did that," she whispered.

Rick watched her try and pull herself together. He was stunned by the swift change in her mood, and yet he wasn't. "Why not?" he asked, hanging on to his temper by a thread.

"You know very well why not," she muttered as she slipped off the bed.

Reluctantly, Rick retrieved his jeans, put them on, then lay where he was, watching her. "Tell me anyway," he prodded.

"For starters, we hardly even know each other."

"We're also engaged."

"Like that counts!"

"It does to me." Rick had no sooner said the words, than he realized they were true. This might have started out as a joke, but somewhere along the way he had stopped viewing it as that. He'd started thinking of it, albeit, unconsciously, as a way to Caroline's heart. Now that they'd made love, he was even more sure he wanted her in his life.

She turned her back on him and began to talk to herself as she hunted around for her shoes. "So I made a mistake," she muttered to herself encouragingly as she bent to look under his bed. She surfaced with one pump, and soon found the other. "I've always learned from my mistakes."

Rick watched her struggle into her pumps. "Why are you so hyper?"

Caroline whirled on him and looked relieved to find him mostly dressed, as well. "Because I don't do things like this!"

"Don't make love?" Rick asked lazily, wondering if she knew how pretty she looked with her bittersweet chocolate hair all tousled, her lips all red and her blouse still half off.

"I don't have love affairs." Caroline looked down at the tricky front clasp as she tried to refasten her bra.

The way her hands were trembling, she'd never manage it. Rick brushed her hands aside and fastened it on one try. "Considering the dry old men you usually keep company with, it's no surprise."

She knocked his hands aside and stepped back, fastening her blouse as she went. "Don't comment on my beaux."

"Why?" He glanced at her in the mirror as she tucked her blouse into her skirt. "Afraid I might speak the truth?"

"I had a moment of weakness." Caroline brushed the wrinkles out of her jacket as best she could, then strode out of the bathroom, found her purse and began to brush her hair. "It won't happen again."

"You call what we just shared a moment of weakness?" Rick had expected Caroline to have trouble with what they'd done, but he hadn't expected her to lie about it.

"What would you call it?" she demanded.

That was easy. Rick grinned. "I'd call it magic."

Caroline sighed, looking more upset than ever. "We just had sex," she said. "Don't make more of it than there was."

Rick's heart pounded so hard against his ribs they hurt. "Meaning what? You won't?" he asked bitterly, stung by the quick way she dismissed him.

Caroline nodded grimly. "You got it."

Chapter Six

"You're late," Marjorie said as Rick joined them at the Confederate House Restaurant in River Oaks. Rick glanced around, barely noticing the tasteful decor and abundant flowers as he searched the room for Caroline.

Not seeing her, he bent to kiss Marjorie's cheek. "I know and I'm sorry." He went back to scanning the crowd of Houston's social elite and the Hollywood celebrities who had dropped everything and flown in to attend the engagement party Marjorie was giving for her daughter.

"Traffic?"

"A mix-up of plans." Rick tensed as he caught a whiff of Caroline's signature perfume. He turned toward the scent. Caroline was beside him. The first thing he noticed was that she'd had her hair done. The silky bittersweet chocolate strands were coiffed in an elegant chignon that emphasized the symmetry and beauty of her features. To his irritation, he saw she'd gone ahead with her plans to wear the Maxwell Lord colors of pearl gray and dusty rose. And she'd probably done so just to irritate him, he thought, though he should have known better than to try and teach an ice princess like Caroline the difference between business and pleasure. He should have known, from the chemistry sizzling between them, that they wouldn't be able to stop with just a few kisses. He should have known they'd end up making love in his apartment. But he hadn't. And now he had to pay the price.

Rick looked into Caroline's eyes, deliberately holding her gaze, daring her to look away. "I was just explaining to your mother why I was late."

Caroline smiled, but the expression didn't reach her eyes. "Bad manners?" she guessed.

"Mix-up of plans," he corrected, lacing an arm about her waist, both because he felt the deep need to publicize his claim on her and because he knew it would irk her unbearably to be held so close to his side. "I was supposed to pick you up, darling," he reminded her.

"No, you weren't." She placed the flat of her hand on his chest and exerted a distancing pressure he ignored. "We were supposed to meet here, remember?"

"No. I don't."

"Now, now, dears." Marjorie hushed them both with a censuring look. "Don't argue."

"I can't help it, Mother. Everything this man does is—" Realizing how much she'd given away, Caroline stopped herself abruptly.

"Everything is what?" Marjorie asked.

Caroline shook her head. "Nothing." She tried but failed to suppress a beleaguered sigh. "Rick, let me introduce you around."

"Good idea." Rick smiled at Marjorie. "We'll talk later," he promised.

Marjorie smiled back. "I'll count on it."

"Must you do that?" Caroline said as they walked away.

Rick didn't know why exactly but he delighted in provoking her. Maybe because of the fire that flashed in her eyes or the spirit she showed when she was challenged. Maybe just because it was the one sure way to get and hold her attention. "Do what?" he asked innocently.

"Charm every woman in sight."

He used the hand on her spine to turn her to face him. "Is that what you think I'm doing?"

Caroline propped her hands on her waist. "I don't know what you're doing."

Yes, Rick thought, she did. They both did. He was falling in love with her and she knew it. She just didn't want to admit it. She didn't want her life to become that complicated. "Charming you?" he asked.

"Hardly," Caroline huffed.

"Making love, then." Oh, how he'd like to do that again! Even in the prim pink-and-gray suit, she looked sexy as hell.

Showing none of the vulnerability she had evidenced earlier, Caroline said, "Will you be quiet?"

"Why?" Rick shrugged. He liked the way the color flowed into her cheeks whenever she became emotional. "We're engaged."

"Not so loud! Rick, please—" Caroline all but moaned. "We *discussed* what happened earlier."

"'Discussed,'" he echoed, recalling the way she'd fled his bed, and then walked out on him as if nothing monumental had happened. "Is that what you call it? A discussion?" *His* life had been changed forever.

"Yes." Her spine was ramrod straight, her jaw defiant.

"Well, I don't," Rick said heavily, wishing Caroline would be honest about her feelings this once. Taking her by the shoulders, he moved her off to a deserted corner. "You lectured, you accused. You didn't listen to a damn thing I had to say. Or even want me to work a word in edgewise."

Caroline's slender body stiffened defensively. "That's because I knew you would rationalize what we'd done."

"Not rationalize. Justify. There's something between us, Caroline. Something—" He was about to say *real,* when Hugh walked up.

"Glad you could make it, old buddy." Hugh patted Rick on the shoulder with a put-on grace. "I was worried for a while that you might not show up."

"Oh, I'll be wherever Caroline is," Rick assured Hugh. He turned back to Caroline with a telling look. "And I'll especially be there when she needs me to be." *Whether she wants me to be or not.*

"I see." Hugh looked displeased. "Caroline?" Hugh continued smoothly. "If Rick would be so kind as to excuse us, I need to speak to you. Alone."

RICK WATCHED CAROLINE walk away with Hugh trotting at her side like some lovesick watchdog. Caroline might have been fooled by Hugh's nerdy manner. Not Rick. He knew a shark when he saw one, and old Hugh there was just biding his time. One way or another, Hugh was determined the company would be his, and would stop at nothing to get it. But not if he had anything to do about it, Rick decided.

He walked over to rejoin the two of them before any intimate chitchat could begin. He was joined by two other members of the board, Miriam Humphrey and Cy Rutledge. Rick knew both Miriam and Cy held ten percent voting shares of Maxwell Lord stock. And though Miriam might seem only interested in the products she developed in her lab, and Cy the slant of his newest ad campaigns, both were extremely interested in the company as a whole, and in Caroline.

"Caroline, I'm so happy you're getting married," Miriam Humphrey said. The chemist kissed Caroline's cheek. "I know it's what Max would have wanted for you."

"I'm happy for you, too, of course, Caroline, but I'm also concerned," Cy Rutledge countered frankly. "Are you sure a new marriage and a new job isn't going to be too much to handle simultaneously?" He paused discreetly. "Perhaps you could grow into the job, wait until you're more settled. The board could elect another president, on an interim basis of course."

"Wait a minute," Caroline said. "The last time we talked you said I could count on your vote, Cy."

"That's true," Cy admitted reluctantly. "But that was before I talked to Hugh. He's concerned about you trying to do too much all at once. I know how tough the first year of marriage is for anyone, and I have to agree it would be a lot of stress all at once. No one on the board wants to see you jeopardizing your health or emotional well-being.''

"On the other hand," Rick chimed in helpfully, ignoring Caroline's dark warning look, "Hugh doesn't have that problem as he's not planning to marry anyone at the moment." It was a lousy thing to say and he knew it, but somehow, now, Rick wanted her to care more about him than the presidency.

"True," Cy Rutledge said seriously. "And as Hugh's always worked so closely with Caroline in the past, I'm sure Hugh would do an excellent job—"

"So would I," Caroline cut in firmly. "And if it comes to making a choice between the two, my marriage and my job, I'll choose my job," she said defiantly.

"How do you feel about that?" Miriam Humphrey asked Rick. "Doesn't it bother you, playing second fiddle to Caroline's ambition?"

Rick looked at Caroline. He knew she was depending on him to bail her out. He also knew anything less than total forthrightness with the board members wouldn't wash. "I think if two people are going to get married that their marriage should be their first priority, period," he said.

"Even if it meant Caroline would have to give up her shot at the company presidency, at least for now?" Cy asked, disturbed but not surprised.

Rick noted that Hugh wasn't making much of an effort to bail Caroline out, either, although he could have. "If it came to that, I'd give up my job, too," Rick said, "and opt for something less demanding." He gave Caroline a steady look. "I don't think it'll come to that, though. I think Caroline is the kind of woman who can handle anything she sets her mind to, including her work and a new marriage simultaneously. After all, isn't that what the company presidency is all about? Juggling a number of interests?"

Cy relaxed. Miriam beamed. Caroline let out a slow breath. She continued to hold his eyes. "Thank you, Rick," she said softly.

The chitchat continued several moments longer. Miriam and Cy wandered off. "Hugh—" Caroline began. "We've got to make a final decision on the bonus-gift-with-purchase for the men's line. Why haven't you gotten back to me?"

"Sorry," Hugh said brusquely.

"He's been far too busy stabbing you in the back," Rick said.

Caroline ignored Rick's gibe, although she was uncomfortably aware how true it was. Hugh was out to get the presidency at any cost, including their friendship.

"I've got to have your input tomorrow," Caroline continued to Hugh. "Meet me in my office at three o'clock, so Tony, you and I can go over this."

Hugh frowned. "I already have an appointment, Caroline."

Caroline cut him off with an imperious look. "Be there, Hugh. Or we'll make the decision without you."

Hugh's eyes darkened ominously.

Rick saw the tuxedoed waiters bringing out the pâté. Perfect timing, he thought. Anything to break this up. "Later, Hugh." He turned to Caroline and clasped her hand. "Your mother is waving at us. We'd better go."

"I'M TELLING YOU, Caroline, you are making a big mistake," Hugh said, after a rich Southern meal of steak and shrimp and a dessert of chocolate cake.

Caroline looked behind Hugh, to see if anyone else was in earshot. Thankfully, it was just the two of them outside the powder room.

"Rick is using you. I even know how now," Hugh continued.

Caroline blinked in confusion. "What are you talking about?"

"He has a scheme. A business proposal...."

"Don't you think I should be the one to tell her about that?" Rick said.

Hugh glowered at Rick. "You mean you haven't?"

Her heart beating double time, Caroline turned to Rick. She could see now, in her effort to avoid conflict with Rick, that she had put this off too long. "What's he talking about?" she asked calmly.

Ignoring her question, Rick said simply, "Are you ready to go home?"

She had been. Now, Caroline didn't know if that was such a good idea. She didn't want to be alone with Rick, for fear that what had happened this afternoon would happen again. She'd been weak once. She couldn't afford to be weak again. "I really should stay and say good-night to everyone with Mother."

Rick smiled, but the expression of happiness didn't quite reach his eyes. "We're lovebirds. The guests won't mind if we sneak out a little early."

Caroline sighed. Neither man was making this easy on her. She had to either listen to Hugh tell her how Rick was going to use her or listen to Rick's version of the same. "All right, Rick."

"Caroline..." Hugh said in a reproaching tone.

"We'll talk tomorrow, Hugh," Caroline promised. "Remember. My office. Three tomorrow afternoon."

She and Rick went to the parking lot. "Did you drive?"

"No," she said. "I came with Mother, who ordered a limousine."

"Then I'll take you home."

Caroline thought of the way it had felt to be held in his arms. She thought of his passionate kisses and even more devastatingly sensual lovemaking, and knew she couldn't risk either again and still keep her wits about her. "I don't want to go home," she said stubbornly.

"My place?" He looked hopeful as he unlocked the passenger door of his Jaguar.

Caroline thought of his rumpled sheets and comfortable bed. "I don't think so."

He grinned as if knowing exactly why she was refusing him, and delighting in it. "Then where?" he asked.

Caroline tried without much success to keep the asperity out of her voice. "Why don't you just drive?"

"Because," Rick said softly, "I want to look at your face when I tell you what I have to say."

A chill went down her spine. These were the kinds of conversations that always went from bad to worse. "That bad, huh?" she guessed lightly and got into the car.

He got in on the driver's side, started the car and backed it out, all without responding.

"Where are we going?" she asked.

"Back to the place I'm remodeling."

She thought about the big empty building on Westheimer where she'd found him that afternoon. "Why?"

Rick cut out of their lane and into another, weaving the Jag in and out of the tumultuous Houston traffic as easily as he breathed. "Because you'll have an easier time envisioning it there," he said confidently.

"Envisioning what?"

Rick merely shrugged. "We'll talk later, princess. When I can look into your eyes."

Fine. Be that way, she thought, then sank deeper into her thick cushioned leather seat.

As he drove, she watched him surreptitiously out of the corner of her eye. He looked good in a suit and tie. Damn good. As good as he had looked in the work shirt and jeans today, as good as he had looked in that drenched range coat and starched white tuxedo shirt and bow tie the first night she had met him.

In all the time she had known him, in all the situations, she had never seen him look ill at ease. She admired his ability to keep his chin up and his fears—assuming he had some—to himself. Just as she admired his ability to take his passion where he found it. She wished she could feel as at ease about what they had done this afternoon. But all she could think was for the second time in her life she had opened herself up to possible hurt from a man she really didn't know. An attractive man, certainly, a giving man, but a relative stranger all the same.

Fortunately, she was saved from further ruminating on her reckless behavior earlier in the day by their arrival. Still not speaking, they got out and walked inside past a large atrium-style lobby, a reception desk and then a series of small rooms off several halls, at the end of which was a large utilitarian laundry room. "Okay, I give up. What is it?" she asked.

Rick merely smiled and led her through another door and down another hallway. They looked in on a gym, an indoor swimming pool and track, a beauty salon and sauna.

"This is a full-service, one-day rejuvenating health spa," he finally said. "Men and women will be able to come here and get the works. They'll be picked up at the door by a chauffeured limousine, brought here and pampered head to toe. But—" he paused and smiled at her "—not with just any products, if I have my way."

Beginning to smell a rat, Caroline said, "No?"

"No. The women and men here will be using only Maxwell Lord products."

Caroline stiffened. Hugh had told her she was being used; she hadn't believed him. Fool, she thought. "We already have a distribution system set up, Rick." Mouth tight, she moved away from him.

He moved with her, his steps long and lazy, his hands thrust into the pockets of his trousers. "In order to sell Maxwell Lord products, you have to get people to try them." He waited until he caught her glance until he continued. "Where better than at one of my one-day spas, where they leave you feeling like a million bucks? Think about it, Caroline. Think about all the women who would love to go to The Golden Door but can't afford a week's stay there. They can come here. And they'll leave with a bagful of your products, so they can duplicate the experience at home."

Caroline wanted to hate his idea, but she loved it. "This is what you've wanted from me all along?" Caroline asked, trying without much success to contain her hurt. "My backing in a joint business deal?"

"It's why I tried to get an appointment to see you, yes."

Her world was tilting precariously. She wanted to climb into bed, pull the covers over her head and never get up again. But that was the coward's way out and she wasn't a coward. She would fight her weakness just as she would fight him. So she'd made a mistake, not realizing he was a scheming underhanded opportunist from the outset. She wouldn't do so again. "Take me home, Rick," she said tightly.

"Caroline—" His voice was soft, pleading. He looked at her, begging her to give him a chance, to try and see things from his position.

But it was far too much to ask. Feeling like her heart was breaking, Caroline said, "Just take me home."

Chapter Seven

"How'd you find me?" Caroline asked. She walked briskly out of the store and into the mall.

"The same way everyone else does. I just checked your work calendar and found out you were making a personal appearance at the opening of a new store in Dallas today."

Caroline shot him an arch look. It was only noon and already she was exhausted. The staff of salespeople had started doing makeovers on customers, on an invitation only basis at eight this morning, two hours before the department store officially opened its doors. The crowds had been enormous. Overall, she was very pleased with the way things had gone. She couldn't say as much about her relationship with Rick—if that was what one could call it. "Nothing in this life is ever easy, Rick," she said tiredly, casting him an arch look over her shoulder. "Haven't you figured that out?"

He lengthened his strides to keep up with her. "Why are you so upset?"

Like he didn't know. Caroline race-walked past a jewelry store. "Maybe I just don't want to be used."

He had the gall to look affronted. "Who's using you?"

Who hadn't? she thought angrily. First Armand. Now Rick.

"I suggested something that would be mutually profitable," Rick continued, taking her elbow and steering her out of the path of a sticky-fingered toddler in a stroller. "Your products would have yet another exclusive sales outlet. You could use our profits to finance your new teen cosmetics line."

Caroline shrugged free of his grasp, wishing he didn't look so good in his simple denim work shirt and jeans. "I thought I had made it clear I don't want to go into business with you."

Rick backed her up against a flagstone wall near the mall exit. "If you're talking about the silent treatment you gave me on the drive home last night..."

Both hands clasping the handle, Caroline held her briefcase in front of her knees. "That'd be the one."

Rick rested an outstretched hand on the wall beside her head. He leaned close and murmured in her ear, "I figured you were just mulling over the proposition, thinking about all the angles."

She was irritated by the fact that she could feel the warmth emanating from his outstretched arm. She could recall only too well how it had felt to be held against him, with that same arm wrapped around her, holding her close. She tipped her head up and met his beseeching gaze head-on. "You seem to have considered all the angles yourself. But then that's no surprise, is it?" She turned abruptly, accidentally on purpose whacking his thigh with her briefcase.

He swore and stepped back. She continued on her path to the exit, her high heels clicking on the lacquered flagstone floor. He overtook her easily, despite her hurried pace and skidded to a halt in front of her. Jamming his hands on his waist, he demanded, "What's really bugging you? Is it the fact Hugh knew about my plans first?"

Her own temper was simmering. Caroline favored him with a sugary smile and asked sweetly, "How *did* he find out, anyway?"

Rick shrugged. "It's no secret. I pitched the idea to Hugh, through my attorneys, weeks ago. He turned me down flat. Then I talked to Tony. He, too, turned me down. Both were reluctant to venture into unchartered territory. Then I tried to see you. But was turned down by your secretary. Apparently, Hugh warned her I might call and told her in no uncertain terms that you were not to be bothered. He had already acted on the company's behalf."

"Damn Hugh. He has no right to screen my calls."

"I tried to tell Sue Ellen that. But he'd done such a good job convincing her my company was really just a clever con, she wouldn't budge." Rick paused. "I figured if I could just talk to you once, face-to-face..."

"Which is why you masqueraded as a caterer?"

Rick nodded.

"I don't get it. With all the trouble, why didn't you just go to one of Estée Lauder's companies or Elizabeth Arden?"

His eyes found hers with laser accuracy. "I did, but it always came back to one thing," he said in a soft, low voice. "Maxwell Lord consistently has the best sales and the best product. I want only the best for my new spas."

"Why didn't you just tell me all this in the beginning?" she asked in a strangled voice, aware they'd stopped walking.

"That was the original plan. But then I found out you were having trouble with regards to winning the company presidency. Helping you achieve your goal became my top priority. If either Hugh or Tony won, I'd never be able to get what I wanted.''

"Meaning what, exactly? That you thought you could deal with me?" Caroline ground out.

"You're a better business person than either Tony or Hugh. Tony is too shortsighted, Hugh too self-serving. You're also reported to be very fair. I figured once you were really in a position to help me out, that you would at least hear me out."

"Well, it seems you've gotten what you wished," Caroline said.

"Not really," he said. "I can't figure out why you're so upset with me. You're a business-minded person, with enough vision and imagination to know a sure thing when you see it." He paused, studying her face. "So why don't you want to bet on me?"

"Because I don't like being used!" she said hotly.

"I'm not using you," Rick repeated firmly.

He said that with such candor, she could almost believe him. Almost. "Honestly, Rick," she began with a weariness that went all the way to her soul. "Give me some credit. I'm not twenty-one anymore. I've heard that line before."

His dark brows lowered like thunderclouds over his eyes. "When?"

Her briefcase was beginning to feel heavy. She set it down between them. Resting her hands on the peplum waist of her suit jacket, she said, "When I was twenty, I went to Europe for the summer. Did you know that?"

He shook his head.

"The plan was for me to stay with a tour," she recited in a wry voice. "Instead, I ran off with a thirty-one-year-old man I met at a museum."

"A stuffy old curator?" Rick said hopefully.

"Tour guide," she corrected. "Try sexy, half French, half Scandinavian."

For a moment, he actually looked jealous, but the emotion faded from his expression almost as soon as it appeared.

"Gorgeous, huh?" he prompted in a bored tone.

"In a word—yes," Caroline replied tightly.

"And?"

"And I married him. My father was furious when he found out I'd eloped with a man eleven years my senior, a man I'd just met. And suspicious, because it was so unlike me not to include the family in what should have been the happiest day of my life. So he made a few phone calls to prominent friends of his in France and found out Armand was a fortune hunter.

"He telephoned me in Paris, demanded I have the marriage annulled immediately and come home. When I refused—I just couldn't believe Armand only wanted me for what I could give him financially—my father disowned me. He said as long as I was married to that fortune hunter I couldn't come home again. He didn't want anyone in the States knowing about my foolishness.''

Rick's eyes gentled in such a way she was tempted to seek out his broad chest and strong arms for comfort. Only her pride kept her stubbornly in place opposite him. "What'd your mother think?" Rick asked.

Caroline shrugged. "Mother thought the same thing I did. That it was all highly romantic." Which explained, Caroline thought, a little bit about why she'd been so foolish in the first place. She had a little of her very foolish, extremely overromantic and oversentimental mother in her. "But she agreed that the matter should be kept quiet, until they saw how things went."

"So what happened next?" Rick asked softly. He took her elbow in hand, picked up her briefcase and led her over to a wooden bench by the door. They sank down on it.

Caroline rested her elbow on the back of the bench and turned to face him. Their knees bumped as she swiveled in her seat. She pulled them back, but the tingle from the contact stayed with her. "I spent the rest of the summer in Europe, and my father sent us papers, letting me know I had been disinherited."

Caroline formed her lips in a parody of an accepting smile. "And that, it seemed, was the end of the road for my charming new husband," she said lightly. "Armand didn't say much, but I could tell he was very angry. He asked me that night if I thought Max would ever change his mind. I said no. The next morning I woke up in our hotel room in Paris. My money and credit cards were all gone." Her mouth tightened, in anger. "He even absconded with my passport. I had to call home and beg my father to bail me out. Which he did, but not before delivering a blistering lecture on common sense, and my lack of it when it came to men."

"Which is why you've never dated anyone handsome or charming since, I suppose."

Caroline stiffened and rose to her feet. "Being married for my money once was quite enough, thank you. It's not a humiliation I care to have pounded into my consciousness again."

Rick rose, picking up her briefcase as he did so. He handed it over. Their hands touched briefly as he released his grip on the handle, and Rick looked into her eyes. "If that's the way you feel, then he ruined you in more than one way."

Even though his words were casually uttered, they had a disturbing ring of truth. Her head was pounding. Her heart ached. And yet she wanted nothing more than to walk forward, into his arms, and let him kiss her and love her until the past went away. "Please," she said, "no more dime-store psychoanalysis."

"Want the real thing, hmm?" he teased, trying, she supposed, to lighten her mood.

"What I want," she corrected, in a mocking tone of voice designed to put his teeth on edge, "is to be left alone."

"No, you don't," Rick disagreed amiably. "You knew when I left you at your doorstep last night, that I would find you today, even if it meant tracking you down through your secretary. And you knew that once I found you, I would follow you and persist.... There's still a lot I don't know about you. And vice versa. But time'll take care of that—you'll see."

Caroline lifted her head and looked at him. There was no reason the world should come skidding to a stop every time he entered her hemisphere, and yet it did. Everything stopped. All she could think about when she was near Rick was Rick.

Rick was even right about her fantasies, although she'd walk on a bed of red-hot coals before she let him know that. She had secretly yearned to have him find her today. And that wasn't all she had dreamed about last night as she had tossed and turned in her big lonely bed in her big lonely house. She had dreamed he had not only found her, but made wild passionate love to her again. But she had been down this road before....

"Let me put this so you can understand it, Rick. You are wasting your time with me."

He grinned, not the least bit dissuaded by her cool tone and icy gaze. "Why don't you let me be the judge of that?"

Caroline inhaled a short breath. "I haven't changed my mind about the spas," she said.

"Even if the profits will finance the development of the new teen cosmetics line?"

"I'll find another way to do that," Caroline said firmly.

Rick shrugged, looking completely unfazed. "So we'll drop the subject."

"Just like that?" She glared at him suspiciously, her heart pounding. He was wearing that after-shave again...the one that made him smell like a pine forest after a winter rain.

"At least for today," Rick said.

She stalked away from him, pushed open the glass exit door and stormed through it. "I knew there was a catch to this!" He wasn't giving up, merely working on a new tact.

"Caroline—"

She waved him off. "No time, Rick. I've got to get back to work. I've got a business to run."

"SO WE'LL DEFINITELY include the shaving cream and the after-shave for the new men's line in the bonus-gift-with-purchase," Hugh said later that same day. He typed the information into the laptop computer in front of him. "Along with the samples of lip sun-block, soap and pocket combs."

"Right, the hair gel is out," Caroline said. She looked at Tony, who was flipping through a stack of photos of female models from a modeling agency. "You're sure you can get the samples of shaving cream shipped in time, Tony?"

Tony paused over a picture of a particularly luscious redhead. "Uh—positive." He looked on the back, saw the name of the model and made a note of it on the pad in front of him, then drew a heart around that.

Knowing Tony's one-track mind, Caroline pressed on. "You checked with the plant?"

"Yes." Tony looked up, his expression serious for once. "Kansas said it was no problem. They've fixed their problem on the manufacturing line and are now on their regular production schedule again."

"Well, keep on them," Caroline said. "We're running close to deadline and I don't want any screwups with the launch of the new men's line."

"No problem," Tony assured her. "Is that it for today?"

Caroline nodded. "Yes."

The two men filtered out. Rick sauntered in. Caroline's heart was pounding. She waited until he had closed the door behind him before she spoke. "I thought we had finished our conversation this morning," she said. She wished she didn't feel so ridiculously happy and excited.

Rick shrugged and sat on the edge of her desk. He had changed into a black tweed blazer and tie and looked ready for an evening out on the town. "We just took a time-out," he said with a smile.

The buzzer on the intercom sounded. Caroline reached over and pressed the speakerphone. "Yes?"

"Your mother is on her way in. I thought I'd let you know."

"Thanks." She let go of the button and groaned.

"Trouble?" Rick asked.

"You know my mother. Is she ever anything but?"

Rick's smile lit up his whole face. "You're a funny woman, Caroline."

She warmed at the all-too-real affection she saw in his gaze. She had the sense Rick liked her, flaws and all. She didn't quite know how to handle that, any more than she knew how to rein in her own impulsive nature. She told herself to keep her guard up, and not be a fool. "Funny, how?"

Rick got up to restlessly prowl her elegantly appointed office. He circled around behind her swivel chair, put both hands on her shoulders and began to massage them.

"You don't want to see your mother but you'll see her anyway."

"I can't turn her away!" Caroline exclaimed, incensed.

"See?" Rick's hands worked their magic on the rigid muscles in her shoulders, turning them from granite to pudding. "You're caring one minute. Stubborn as a mule the next." He leaned over her and kissed her forehead lightly.

Caroline closed her eyes, knowing she should get up, or at least make him stop this seductive massage, but it just felt so good.

"Really, Caroline, you might have let me know where you were off to this morning!" Marjorie stormed into Caroline's office. She stopped and smiled at Rick. "I'm trying to plan a wedding, for all the help you're giving me!"

Caroline sighed. She stood and pushed away from Rick. Pacing the room like a caged tiger, she said, "You know I have business obligations, Mother. I can't just walk out on them, wedding or no. And with the launch of the men's line coming up—"

Marjorie waved her to silence. "First of all, it's nearly five o'clock. I happen to know you've already put in a very full day. Sue Ellen assures me there's nothing vital on your calendar that would prevent you from leaving the office at the normal time, like everyone else. At least tonight. Furthermore, it seems to me if Rick was important to you, you'd want to make the time to help plan your own wedding, Caroline."

"What did you want to see me about?"

"What else? We need to complete your wedding plans."

The tension that had been plaguing Caroline came back full force. "It's still a month away, Mother." The launch for the new men's line was in another two weeks. "There's no rush."

"I'm afraid there is, darling. My producer called this morning to remind me to begin memorizing lines for the miniseries. It begins shooting in a month and they want me to get fitted for costumes. We haven't even selected *your* dress!"

"In that case, I don't mind putting my wedding off," Caroline said, trying hard to disguise her relief. At last, something was going her way!

"I do." Rick had the devil in his eyes. "I think we've wasted quite enough time already. Besides, how much time can it take to select a wedding dress?"

Thanks heaps, she telegraphed with her eyes, in a look only he could see.

"I'm with Rick," Marjorie said. "As long as the two of you are in love and have already set the date, there's no reason to delay, even if I have to prepare both for my new film and your wedding simultaneously. Unless... You haven't changed your mind, have you, Caroline?"

"Heavens no, Mother!" Caroline said, imagining the havoc that would cause among the members of the board.

"Well, that's a relief!" Marjorie pressed a hand to her heart.

"REALLY, CAROLINE, there's no need to frown!"

"I hate trying on dresses." Especially romantic floor-length wedding dresses that were inclined to make her feel all weepy and nostalgic. She was too smart to be influenced by store-bought romanticism, wasn't she? She knew couples didn't really live happily ever after, no matter how blissful their courtships were. And for couples like she and Rick, who fought as much as they got along...well, there could be no hope their romance would have a storybook-perfect ending.

"Well, you shouldn't hate trying on dresses," Marjorie scolded. "It's fun! Besides—" she studied her daughter in the mirror, smiling with maternal pride ''—you look beautiful.''

That was just the problem, Caroline thought. She *did* look beautiful in every single dress she had tried on, and she had already tried on half a dozen. It would be so easy to be caught up in the fantasy of a real wedding and a real reception . . . to let herself dream about saying ''I do'' to Rick . . . to go off with him on some fabulous honeymoon.

But it wasn't going to happen. Once the board voted her the new president, the engagement would be delayed for work-related reasons, then called off. She intended to drag her heels as much as possible. The less they did, the less she'd have to undo.

''What is it you don't like about the dress?'' the saleswoman asked.

Caroline glared at herself in the salon mirror. ''It's the leg-of-mutton sleeves, I guess. They make me feel like I got stuck in a time warp.'' A time warp where all women got married and lived happily ever after. Except her.

''Why don't you try something simple and sophisticated?'' Rick asked from the door of the bridal salon. ''Something more . . . Caroline.''

Caroline whirled toward him in a rustle of satin and lace. Damn him for not staying away. Damn her for being secretly glad to see him every time he showed up. She was desperately afraid his devotion to her was something she could get used to.

Marjorie's face had lit up when Rick crashed the fitting session. "You may be right," she said thoughtfully.

"Hey!" Caroline pointed an accusing finger at her fiancé. "You're not supposed to be in here."

"Caroline's right, Rick," Marjorie said as her future son-in-law crossed to Caroline's side and wrapped a hand around her waist. "It's bad luck to see the bride in her wedding dress before the wedding."

Caroline whispered beneath her breath. "In that case, stay. We need all the roadblocks to the nuptials we can get. My mother's going at the plans like a steamroller. She can't be stopped."

He grinned. "Don't worry, princess. I'm here to save you."

"I don't need rescuing," she whispered back.

"Yes, you do," he teased. "And I'm just the man to do it." Rick turned to her mother, "Is this the dress she'll be wearing when she marries?" he asked innocently enough.

"No," Marjorie and the saleswoman said in unison.

"Then in that case it doesn't matter, does it?" He turned back to her, his eyes like dark green steel. "I have to speak to you alone."

When they were alone, there was always trouble. "Maybe after this—"

"Now, Caroline." Giving her no chance to dissent, he swung her up in his arms, flowing skirts and all and strode in the general direction of the dressing room.

Feeling treacherously off balance, Caroline laced her arms about his neck and held on for dear life, trying not to notice how strong his shoulders were, how firm his chest. She was throbbing all over, as if her body had a million pulse points, all converging together into one.

"Excuse us a minute, ladies," he called over his shoulder.

Caroline held her tongue until he had set her down in the middle of a dressing room. "That was quite a display."

"Wasn't it?" He seemed pleased.

"I hope you're finished—"

He shot out an arm and clamped it to the doorknob, preventing her escape. "Not quite."

Caroline backed up a pace, terribly afraid she knew what was coming next. "What's so urgent it can't wait?"

Rick smiled and wrapped his arms around her. "This." His lips were warm and firm against hers. Not harsh and commanding, in the way she would have expected, but sweetly coaxing, loving. His tenderness was almost her undoing. Fortunately, there was an audience just outside the door. *Lord, she was letting it happen again!* Was she really that easily seduced? Fooled? Bamboozled?

"Oh, Caroline, I've been missing you," Rick murmured as his seeking mouth made a lazy trail down her neck.

Tingles of fire swept through her. Her breasts throbbed. Her knees weakened. Lower still, moisture gathered like morning dew on the grass. "Rick—" She put a hand to his chest, aware she was treacherously close to giving him everything he wanted.

He tightened his hold possessively. All the yearning she felt deep in her heart came through loud and clear in his low, sexy voice. "I know, I know. I shouldn't. We shouldn't. And maybe you're right. I can't help it, Caroline. You're just so beautiful and smart and stubborn and sexy."

He shook his head, as if amazed at what he was saying, then continued in a tone that was even more private and honest. "I can't stop thinking about you." His eyes meshed with hers, held. "About us." He clasped her hand in his and knitted their fingers together tightly. "I want us to go away together." His callused palm scored hers with heat. "I want to find out if what we shared the other night is real."

He was moving too fast for her, but then that was Rick. When he saw something he wanted, he went right after it. But would he tire of her? And want to move on to something...someone else. Unlike her, he had not stuck with just one business, but jumped from one to the next at whim. She didn't want to end up like one of his other businesses, on the back burner somewhere.

"Promise me you'll go, Caroline. Promise me you'll give us a chance."

"I want to, Rick."

"But?" The word was clipped.

"I can't."

"Why not?" Impatience replaced understanding.

"I've got to stay here and take care of business. The beginning days of my presidency will be crucial." The real truth was that she couldn't let herself trust him that much. She couldn't let herself weaken.

Another heartbeat passed. "I won't give up," Rick warned.

"I know." The surprise was that she had stopped wanting him to give up.

Chapter Eight

Rick knew there was going to be hell to pay when Caroline found out what he'd been up to, and he wasn't disappointed. Her hazel eyes flashed daggers when she strode into the boardroom and saw him. Amazing, he thought, that anyone could look so overwhelmingly sexy in such a prim little navy suit and pearls.

Color flowed into her classically beautiful face. "Who invited him here?" Caroline asked both Hugh and Tony, her eyes still fastened on Rick.

"Tony and I did," Hugh murmured, as if it were the most natural thing in the world. When in reality, Rick thought, it was just Hugh trying to save his own skin—and his relationship, if one could even call it that, with Caroline. Hugh knew from their mutual conversation and tour yesterday evening that Tony liked Rick's proposal, now that he'd thought about it some more, and was determined to take it forward. Now, the board would be more likely to keep an open mind. Hence, Hugh probably figured it would be politic to be in on whatever happened there. Unfortunately, Hugh also thought this business deal was all Rick was really after. But nothing could have been further from the truth, Rick thought.

He wanted Caroline, heart and soul, and somehow, someway, he was going to make her feel that way about him, too. He knew she desired him. That was in her eyes every time she looked at him. And she trembled when he touched her. The two of them were meant to be together. Rick was sure of it. First he would take care of business. Maybe if Caroline saw he had nothing further to gain from his association with her, and still wanted to be with her, then she would begin to trust him.

"I thought the board should know what Rick's up to," Hugh said when Marjorie Lord, Miriam Humphrey and Cy Rutledge all filtered into the room. The newcomers took their places at the other end of the table.

Caroline glanced down at the printed agenda in her hand. Her cheeks glowed with unusually high color. "You invited him to give a pitch?" she whispered, looking all the more upset, as she slid into her chair and scooted it closer to the table.

"The same courtesy I would extend to any other entrepreneur who had a product that could potentially benefit our company."

Tony cut in amiably, siding with Rick and Hugh. "Frankly, Caroline, I'm surprised you didn't invite Rick to make this pitch yourself," he said.

Caroline drew Tony aside. In a voice barely above a whisper, she accused, "You're getting back at me for placing those ads, aren't you?"

Tony only smiled. "I told you, you weren't the only one who could play dirty, sis. And as it happens, this is going to make me look very good to the board. Thanks to Rick, I'm learning it's not as hard to take business risks as I thought. Particularly when they're bound to work out."

Her jaw set testily, Caroline retorted, "Well, I make it a point never to mix business and pleasure."

Tony grinned mischievously, as if enjoying her discomfiture, and sat back in his chair. "Then you've got yourself a dilemma, don't you, sis, 'cause Hugh and I both want to do business with Rick."

Caroline glared at Rick. "How dare you do this to me?" she said under her breath.

"You knew I would."

"No," she said, her tone clipped, "I didn't."

"Then you should have." Rick gave her a hard look. "When it comes to business, I never give up, and certainly not without a fight."

Her pretty mouth tightened into a thin line. "If it's a fight you want—"

"Are we about ready to get started?" Marjorie asked restlessly. "I've got an appointment with my dialect coach this morning, and I'd like to go shopping before we meet."

Rick had to admire the way Caroline kept her cool in spite of the unbusinesslike way her mother regarded this meeting and, Rick suspected, all of Maxwell Lord business. Caroline was right; Marjorie's priorities were a bit out of whack. On the other hand, Marjorie was right about Caroline needing more of a personal life. From what he'd seen, all she did was work.

"Yes, we are. Rick, since you're here, you may as well go first," Caroline said coolly.

Rick grinned at her, even though she didn't grin back, then stood and walked over to an easel. The board listened intently to his pitch.

"I love it!" Marjorie said, when he'd finished.

"Sounds promising," Miriam Humphrey said.

"Very promising," Tony agreed.

Hugh was silent, waiting, Rick figured, to see which way the corporate winds were blowing before jumping on either bandwagon.

"I don't know. It sounds awfully risky to me," Cy Rutledge intervened, with his customary reserve.

"Cy's right," Caroline said, pausing to look at the board members seated around her. "If we attach our name to this, and Mr. Cassidy's venture fails, then it'll be a black mark on our record."

Rick hadn't really expected Caroline to back him, but he resented her doom-and-gloom attitude. Briefly, his eyes connected with hers. "I think that's a moot point," he said quietly. "I don't intend to fail." He took a deep breath and made eye contact with each and every member of the board. "But you needn't take my word for it. Why not experience it firsthand for yourself, then decide? I invite all of you to be my guests."

"Good idea," Miriam Humphrey said, looking pleased. "After all, a single hands-on experience will tell us volumes more than any presentation."

Cy Rutledge frowned. "If we're going to do it, I think we should all go at once."

"The sooner the better," Hugh remarked.

Rick interpreted that to mean, "The sooner we get rid of Rick, the better."

"I think we should all go together, too," Marjorie put in. She adjusted the fox stole around her shoulders. "That way we can make a real party of it!"

"Sounds good to me," Rick agreed. "Caroline?"

Outwardly, Caroline looked calm but Rick knew enough about her to realize that underneath she was about ready to explode. He was sorry he was responsible for the stress. He wasn't sorry he'd followed through on his plan. His plan was a good one. It would profit them all. When Caroline calmed down, she would see that.

"It's up to the board," Caroline said evenly.

The members chatted among themselves. In the end it was Tony who finally spoke for the group, "You're on, Rick. Show us what you can do."

"YOU LOOK STRESSED," Rick said after the meeting. He followed Caroline down to her office on the executive floor.

Her high heels made a sharp staccato on the polished marble floor. "*Frazzled* is the word I think you're looking for. And yes, Rick, I am."

"Good."

She shot him a sharp look over her shoulder and continued racing down the hall, her hips swaying provocatively beneath the trim skirt.

Rick tried but couldn't quite pry his eyes from the flexed muscles in her calves. She had strong sexy legs. He could still recall how they'd felt wrapped around his waist. And he wanted to feel them there again.

"Then my rejuvenating spa will make you feel even better," he said. He stalked past her secretary, followed her into her office and slipped past before she could slam the door in his face. She ended up closing them in.

She whirled to face him. Her feet were planted slightly apart and her eyes were glittering. "*I* have no plans to go."

Caroline never gave an inch without a fight. Luckily he liked fighting with her. He liked seeing the hot excited color pour into her cheeks and seeing her hazel eyes flash with passion and her soft lips pout. When she pouted, he wanted to kiss her. Striding lazily past her, he cleared a place and sat on the edge of her desk. "You have to go."

Caroline swiveled slowly to face him. "Why?"

"Because everyone else on the board is going. And as interim president, that means you should, too."

Caroline regarded him thoughtfully, reminding him a little of a lioness on the warpath. Tossing her mane of bittersweet chocolate hair—hair that for once had not been restrained in some prim little ponytail at the back of her neck—she stalked past him to the window. She fiddled with an earring and kept her back to him. "I think you should know right now I am not planning to vote yes on your proposal, Rick.''

"Because I'm your fiancé and you think it'll be viewed as nepotism by the board? Or because you don't trust me?"

"Both."

Rick closed the distance between them. "If you're going to vote no, at least do it based on your experiences at my spa. Don't crucify me just because you're angry at me for persisting."

"Don't tell me how to feel! I have every right to be angry with you." Caroline stormed past him with another lofty toss of her head. She whirled to face him. "You went to Tony and Hugh again when I'd already told you no. I felt like a fool, having Tony introduce your proposal to the board."

"What difference does it make who proposed it?" Rick asked in frustration. "It's a good proposal."

Caroline said nothing.

"Come on," he said, exasperated. "You didn't really expect me to give up without a fight, did you?"

Caroline threaded both hands through her hair, pushing it off her face. "That's the problem, Rick," she said dryly, spinning away from him in a drift of wildflower perfume. "Around you, I *never* know what to expect."

So much the better, he thought. He liked an element of surprise. It kept every relationship fresh. "So show up tomorrow," he urged. "Or better yet, enjoy the full experience and let me send a limo to pick you up. After you've been pampered from head to toe, then decide whether Maxwell Lord wants in on the ground floor of my venture or not."

Caroline sent him a wary look. "I suppose I had better go, since all the other board members will be there, as well," she conceded with obvious reluctance.

"WHAT HAPPENED to you?" Miriam Humphrey asked shortly after eight the following morning when Caroline strolled into Rick's Place, trying not to feel too refreshed from the orange juice, flaky croissants and hot, strong coffee she'd had on the limousine drive over.

"I was gardening," Caroline replied. She knew she was a mess. Determined to really put Rick's one-day rejuvenating spa to the test, she had awakened early and gone for a run, then spent another hour digging in the rose garden sans gloves. She was hot and sweaty and in desperate need of a bath. She was wearing old sweats, which were hopelessly stained with both grass and mud.

As usual, Miriam looked like she was in dire need of a beauty salon. Caroline's mother looked like she had just stepped out of one. Tony, Hugh and Cy all fared worse. None of the three had shaved or showered, and had come in, in varying degrees of casual dress.

"Rick promised we'd all look like a million bucks by the time his staff had finished with us at eight tonight," Caroline continued affably. "I figured I'd get my money's worth."

Rick joined them in the lobby. His glance scanned her, but no expression was readily identifiable on his face. Rick turned to the others. "Everyone ready?"

Rick pressed a button on the wall. His staff appeared almost instantaneously. "They're all yours," he said, to the uniformed group.

First on the agenda was a private counseling session with a member of the staff. Caroline half expected Rick to meet with her personally, but she was assigned a pleasant young woman instead. They went over her wish list. Caroline chose one-on-one sessions with a nutritionist, a personal trainer and a wardrobe consultant. She also asked to have her hair and nails done. Her old clothes were whisked away and she was outfitted in plain white sweats bearing the spa logo.

The next few hours passed quickly. Caroline saw Rick now and again as he chatted with other board members and guests, but he deliberately left her alone. Caroline told herself firmly she was not miffed by his lack of attention, but it got harder to swallow as the morning wore on. He danced attendance on everyone but her.

Fortunately, her lunch was as wonderful as her breakfast had been. The salad greens were crisp, the dressing light. The chicken vegetable soup was wonderful, rich and filling, as was the whole-grain bread.

"Everything okay?" Rick asked as he stopped by the table where Caroline, Marjorie and Tony were seated.

"Great," Marjorie and Tony both said.

Caroline shrugged, letting Rick know she was not so easily impressed. "I could have used some butter."

"If you wanted it, all you had to do was ask," Rick said. He smiled at her and walked away.

"Being a little hard on him, aren't you, sis?" Tony prodded.

Caroline felt her chin thrust out a little farther. She smoothed the Irish linen napkin on her lap. "I just don't like being backed into a corner, that's all." Particularly by a man she was involved with . . . and like it or not, she was involved with Rick.

Marjorie raised a brow.

"Did you sign up for the advanced aerobics workout or the intermediate?" Caroline merely nodded. She looked past Tony to where Rick was standing at Miriam's table. She wished his shoulders weren't so broad. She wished they weren't so well outlined in the formfitting white polo shirt. She wished his trousers didn't do the same for his lower half.

"Advanced," she managed to mumble when she became aware Tony was still waiting for an answer.

Across the room, Rick moved on to talk to some of the staff. Watching him cross his arms against the hardness of his chest, Caroline couldn't help but remember how it had felt to be held against that hard, strong chest of his, the warmth of him flowing through her. The man could make her lose sight of everything . . . and think only of the way his lips felt on hers, so sure and right, and the snug, perfect way their bodies fit together, like two halves of a whole.

Tony grinned. "Well, prepare yourself for the advanced class, sis. It's a killer."

Killer wasn't the word for it, Caroline thought an hour later as she finished the aerobic workout. Sheer torture was more like it. "I won't be able to move tomorrow," she moaned, as her instructor handed her a soft fluffy towel to wipe her face.

"Which is exactly why we're going to put you into the whirlpool for fifteen minutes, then follow it with a full-body massage."

It sounded heavenly. And it was. The whirlpool was private, surrounded by plants and flowers. There was a choice of music. Wrapped in a towel, Caroline went into the massage room and lay face-down on the table. She closed her eyes, thinking Rick was right to be so confident of his success. This was heaven. The spa had something for everyone. For those, like her mother, who hadn't wanted to do aerobics, there had been jazz dancing and tap. Rick even offered fencing and racquetball.

She heard the door open and shut.

Too tired to do much more than mumble a hello to her masseuse, Caroline closed her eyes drowsily, loving the feel of the strong hands that were kneading and pounding and massaging her back. They were wonderful. Warm like fire, soothing like a hot bath, firm and sure.

She moaned and sighed softly.

"Feel good, princess?"

Princess! Caroline turned over and stared up into Rick's face. Her face flamed as she clutched her towel, which had slid treacherously low over the curve of one breast. "You!"

He grinned as she righted her towel. "I wondered how long it would take you to catch on," he drawled.

Caroline rolled her eyes. She tugged the bottom of her towel down, and the top half up. "I should have known," she said.

"Yep, you should have." Rick placed a hand on her shoulder, and pushed her flat on the table. He began working his fingers across her shoulder and down her right arm. "Relax. No one saw me come in. They won't see me leave, either."

"You're sure?"

He nodded. "I'm not out to embarrass you in front of your colleagues. Although I doubt anyone would mind since we're engaged."

Unfortunately, Caroline thought he had a point. It would probably raise more eyebrows if they didn't talk privately. She began to relax.

"So, what do you think so far?" he asked as he kneaded her biceps with slow, heavenly strokes.

"I think it's very nice."

He continued to work out the kinks. When one arm was limp and relaxed, he picked up the other.

"Where did you learn to do this?" she asked.

Rick began working his way from the top of her thigh, down to her knee. "Back in Texarkana." He smiled, confiding, "One of my sisters was a music major. She used to practice her piano for hours on end. Sometimes I would massage her neck and shoulders for her.''

''How many sisters did you have?'' She barely suppressed a groan of contentment as he worked his way past her knee to her calf.

''Seven. I was the youngest. Slip your legs a little farther apart, princess, so I can get under here. Yeah,'' he said. ''You're really tight in your lower thigh. Feel that?''

A wave of longing swept through her, followed by a peculiar lassitude in her whole body. Her limbs were heavy and weak. There was a telltale fluidness in her legs, a tingling in her abdomen, a growing sheen of moisture on the inside of her upper thighs.

''You must've been spoiled rotten,'' Caroline murmured, hoping he couldn't see the way her nipples were beading beneath the thick cotton cloth.

Rick dropped one limp thigh and moved around the table to begin his magic on her other leg. ''All my sisters think so, that's for sure. 'Course, they were the ones that spoiled me.''

Caroline swallowed around the dryness of her throat. ''Are you close to them now?''

''Yep. A few of them don't live in Texas anymore but we all write and call each other and see each other whenever we can.''

"Your family was happy?"

"Yep, in a 'Brady Bunch' kind of way." Looking completely absorbed in his work, Rick massaged the area just beneath her knee. "We didn't have a lot, moneywise," he continued affably. "We all had summer jobs from the time we were old enough to cut lawns, deliver newspapers and babysit. But we were loved and cared for, so the material stuff we didn't have didn't matter much."

"And yet you're very ambitious," Caroline observed.

He shrugged, his hands moving past her knee to her thigh. "When I see something that needs doing, I've got to do it."

"The car wash?" she asked softly.

Rick paused. Knowing she just wanted to talk for a moment, he sat on the edge of the table. Caroline sat up, too. He looked her straight in the eye as he spoke. "They ruined my car, Caroline. A car I had sweated hours to earn the money for. It wasn't the first time they had ruined a car, but I swore it would be the last. I sued 'em, and won, and then took the place over and ran it right."

"And then kept doing that," Caroline said.

"Like I said, when I see something wrong, I have to make it right."

"What about the rejuvenating spa? How'd you get hooked into doing this?"

"One of my sisters had a new baby last year. She complained to me no one pampered *her* anymore. She spent all her time pampering her husband and her child. She wanted to go someplace like The Golden Door, but it was too expensive."

"And so you decided to build her a spa?"

"That's the general idea."

"Heck of a present."

"And a business idea," he agreed.

A comfortable silence fell between them. Suddenly she felt as if she had known him a long time, all her life. She studied him solemnly, wondering wistfully what it would be like to be the sole object of Rick's devotion. "You're really sweet, you know that?" she said softly.

"You haven't experienced the half of it, princess, but you will one of these days," he said.

The look in his eyes made her breath stop. She had never seen such desire. "Rick—" She meant the word as a warning. Nevertheless, it came out as caress.

"You're beautiful, you know that?" He brushed the hair from her face. "So beautiful. Not just outside but inside, too. You're all I think about these days. All I want. All I'll ever want," he whispered.

The vulnerability in his voice got to her the way no smooth seduction technique ever could have.

Caroline knew it wasn't what he'd intended when he had entered the ultraprivate massage room, but she slid her arms around his neck anyway and brought as much of her body as she could against his. The next thing she knew their mouths had locked in a searing kiss and he was stretched out on the massage table beside her, one leg between hers. Holding her tightly, he continued the languorous kiss. Desire swept through her in dizzying waves. Her muscles, deliciously fluid only moments before, now stretched and strained. She arched against him wantonly, no longer caring what common sense dictated, only caring that this never end. "Oh, Rick."

Rick responded hungrily, clasping her close.

He shuddered as her tongue swept his mouth, hotly and voraciously. She could feel the strength of his arousal, pressing against the apex of her thighs, and knew he was just as caught up in the spell as she was.

Needing to feel all of him against all of her, her hands slid beneath the hem of his shirt and moved up and over the bunched muscles of his back and chest. Her fingers slid through the silky mat of hair on his chest, then lower, to the waistband of his pants.

"Damn, Caroline." He caught her hand before she could go farther and held it still against the washboard flatness of his abdomen. Against the side of her palm, she could feel the tight nest of curls. He caught his breath and whispered hoarsely, "If you do that—"

Caroline smiled, liking the fact that for once he was on the edge, fighting his desire. "What, Rick?" she asked softly, fighting his grip and moving her hand a little lower, to bump against the ridge of hot, hard silk. Her heart was pounding. Lower still, she throbbed and grew even damper. She felt empty and she wanted to be filled . . . loved . . . completely overwhelmed and bewitched. "What'll happen, Rick?"

He let out a shaky breath and edged his lower half away from her slightly, so she was no longer touching him in quite so intimate a way. "You know very well what'll happen," he said gruffly. His jade eyes were flashing.

So? she thought as she watched his mouth twist indecisively. She wanted it to happen. Before they could think about the consequences.

But this time Rick had other ideas. His hand clasping hers, he brought it out of his slacks. He slowly, reluctantly lifted his lips from hers. For several moments they stayed just that way, locked together tightly, his forehead resting on hers. She could feel the steady thrumming of his heart, just as she could feel the tension in his legs and the rock-hard ridge of arousal against her thigh. And she knew how much it was costing him not to make love to her then and there.

Rick drew a ragged breath and looked deep into her eyes. "When I make love to you again—and I will make love to you again, Caroline—it's going to mean a commitment," he said.

She could tell by the way he looked at her, that he wanted her more than ever. What surprised her was that she wanted him, too. So much she no longer cared that he might be using her.

"Rick—" It was unfair of him to leave her like this.

"I know what you're thinking—that at this moment you could care less about the consequences of our actions. But I also know that ultimately you want more than a fleeting love affair. Ultimately, Caroline, you want something permanent and enduring. And I do, too." He gently disengaged their bodies and got to his feet. "We made love rashly once, Caroline. We shouldn't do it again."

Caroline released a lengthy sigh and raised up slightly, supporting her weight on her elbows. She wanted to be furious with him. But it was impossible. How could she resent someone for caring about her feelings, long-term?

As her passion and the delicious euphoria that went with it faded, her doubts crept back to the fore. Was it really marriage Rick wanted? Or did he just think that was what she wanted, and was paying lip service to that accordingly? Had he lost interest in her, romantically, now that he'd almost gotten what he wanted? Or had he just had a sudden attack of conscience because he was close to getting his business deal and wanted to make sure nothing soured it? She wasn't sure she wanted to know, not if it would hurt her.

She swept her hands through her hair, slowly restoring order to the dark strands. "You're awfully sure of yourself, aren't you?" she asked with a sigh.

"No, Caroline," Rick corrected softly. "I'm sure of you. And I know what it'll take to make you happy. Believe me," he said heavily, "it isn't this."

Chapter Nine

"I thought you'd be happy for me," Rick began, several days later, after the board had met and voted on Rick's proposal.

"I am." Heart pounding, emotions awhirl with confusion, Caroline slipped into the chair behind her desk.

"It's a real coup," Rick continued, lazily following her into the room.

"I'm sure your spas will be a smashing success," she said coolly.

Rick's eyes scanned her from head to foot, taking in everything from her dangly silver earrings to the demure ladylike way she had crossed her legs at the knee beneath the hem of her pale yellow suit.

"And Maxwell Lord will sell a lot of their products, especially their products for men." He pushed a stack of papers aside, sat on the edge of Caroline's desk and hooked a finger beneath her chin. "So why so glum?"

Because now that you have what you want, I'm afraid you won't need me anymore. "Nothing's wrong. I'm just very stressed." She bounded up out of her chair and moved across the room, into the adjacent lab. Moments later she returned with a crystal bottle. "Did you see this?"

Rick looked at the writing on the gray-and-white faux-marble box. "Max?"

"It's our new men's fragrance, named after my father. It was the last thing he created before he died last year. It debuts with the Maxwell Lord for Men line the day after tomorrow." She uncapped it and handed it over. "What do you think?"

Rick sprayed a little cologne on the backside of his wrist and lifted it to his nose. His eyes widened, then he waved his hand beneath her nose. She inhaled. "I like it," she murmured. "Do you?"

Rick nodded. "It's nice. Brisk. Yet masculine."

"You sound like a wine taster," she teased.

"Sorry." A sexy grin dimpled his face. "I'm not used to reviewing men's cologne, but I do like it."

So do I. Especially on you. "Let's hope the public feels the same way." She recapped the bottle.

"You're worried about it being a success?"

"It's a tribute to my father. If it isn't, I'll feel like I let both him and the company down."

"There's a lot resting on your shoulders, isn't there?" Rick said sympathetically. "So, how are the free-gift-with-purchase packs coming along?"

Caroline sat back in her chair, thinking for a moment how nice it was to simply sit and talk business with Rick. There was no doubt about it. He was an asset to her, businesswise. He was a good sounding board, and the members of the board all liked and respected him. "We're still waiting on the shaving-cream samples to arrive, but Tony assures me they'll reach all the stores this evening, in plenty of time for the official launch, day after tomorrow."

"On Valentine's Day?"

Caroline nodded.

"Doing anything special then?"

"I'll be monitoring the sales results from my office here, from nine in the morning, our time, to midnight."

"Oh."

"You're disappointed in me, aren't you?"

"Well—" he shrugged "—it is Valentine's Day."

"Not for me."

Silence fell between them, less comfortable now. Finally Rick got up and moved restlessly about the room. He stopped in front of her window.

"What are you thinking?" Caroline asked.

"That I wish our engagement were real," he said softly.

Caroline's heart slammed against her ribs. She stared at him, aware these were both the words she'd been longing to hear and at the same time dreading. Was what she could give him still a part of his attraction to her?

She strolled across the room and stood next to him. She slanted her head back beneath his, thinking how unfair it was that he wanted what she feared the most. Intimacy on a no-holds-barred level. "You wouldn't say that if you'd ever been married," Caroline said, keeping her voice light.

"I've been married."

The news hit her with the force of a speeding Mack Truck. Caroline blinked, sure she hadn't heard right. "You? Married?" she croaked.

Rick's sexy grin widened. "Boggles the mind, doesn't it?" he drawled.

She studied his flashing white teeth. "When?"

He glanced out the window before returning his gaze to her face. "A long time ago."

"To whom?" she asked, a tad too impatiently for her taste.

Rick's eyes lit up. He searched her eyes, as if hunting for the first telltale sign of jealousy, but his voice was matter of fact. "Susan Marshall."

"So what happened?"

"Nothing," Rick said candidly, pushing his fingers through the shaggy, tousled layers of his raven-black hair. "That was the problem."

"What do you mean nothing happened?" she demanded, irked he was being so stingy with his information.

"I mean we never saw each other." Rick began to pace the office restlessly. "Rarely had dinner together. Never had a vacation. Our honeymoon lasted all of a day and a half."

"How come?"

Rick paused to examine the potted tree in the corner. He smoothed the leaf between his fingers and thumb. "As I recall, she had a restaurant in Texarkana to run." He let go of the leaf, shoved his hands into the pockets of his suit slacks and turned back to her.

"You divorced her?"

"Yep." Rick stated the fact without remorse.

"Did she fight it?"

His eyes lit up. "You sure are curious," he drawled.

Caroline fought the color that threatened to climb into her face. "I'm supposed to be your fiancée," she announced with deliberate disinterest. "Surely I should know these things."

"In case Hugh comes to you again?" His grin let her know he knew that wasn't her reason for questioning him.

"Of course," she said in a remarkably composed voice.

"Right," he said dryly. He continued with feigned confusion. "Where were we?"

Caroline drew a tranquilizing breath. "You were going to tell me how Susan reacted to the idea of a divorce." Please, let me find out she is *not* still in the picture, Caroline thought.

"She didn't fight it. There was a time when I wished she had," he said quietly, then lifted his broad shoulders in an affable shrug. "Now I'm glad she didn't."

Caroline strolled closer, telling herself she was doing so only because they wouldn't have to shout to be heard. "Did you love her very much?"

"Of course." Rick's glance held hers for a second. "Otherwise I wouldn't have married her."

Caroline discovered the hands she had knitted together were damp with perspiration. "Did she love you?"

"In her own way."

"But?"

"It wasn't enough," Rick said grimly. "She was married to her work. I wanted her to be married to me."

Caroline rolled her eyes. She had heard complaints like this before. "What you really mean is you wanted her to stay at home so she'd be handy to fetch your paper and slippers," she corrected.

"No." His expression hardened. "I just wanted her to have time for us. Time to have a quiet dinner alone at least once a week. Time to make love." He frowned at Caroline's disapproving look. "For instance," he explained, "if I'd have come to her late in the afternoon and wanted to drive down to the Gulf to see the sunset, I would've needed to make an appointment three weeks in advance."

"That's ridiculous."

His eyes gleamed. "Is it?"

What was he up to now? "Yes."

"Ah, I see." He closed the distance between them swiftly, slid his hands around her waist until they overlapped behind her and drew her against him. His eyes gleamed darkly and he gave her an intense, questioning look. "You're telling me if your husband came to you out of the blue and asked you to take a forty-five-minute drive to the beach, just to see the sunset, you'd go." Rick brought one hand around to the front of her and snapped his fingers. "Just like that."

"Well," Caroline hedged, knowing a trick question when she heard one. She flattened a hand against his chest and stepped out of his embrace. "It would depend."

"On what?"

Caroline drew a deep breath. "On whether I had a meeting or—"

"Just like Susan," he remarked disrespectfully. "A workaholic to the bone. I knew it."

Resentment stiffened her from head to toe, forced her shoulders back. "I am not!"

Rick tipped his head to the side and studied her relentlessly. "Then prove it," he challenged with a slow, sexy smile.

Caroline blinked. "What?"

"Have dinner with me. In Galveston." He consulted his watch. "If we leave now, we can just about make the sunset."

His proposal was casual, matter-of-fact. He hadn't touched her. Had suggested nothing the least bit romantic or sexual, and yet she felt danger in every pore. Maybe because she knew he had only to want her to make her want him, too. Her mouth unbearably dry, she stammered, "I—well, I—"

Rick winced, swore and drove a hand through his hair. "Here come the excuses."

"They aren't excuses!" Caroline retorted hotly, not about to take a dressing-down from him when she had endured dozens on the same subject from her flighty mother and her playboy brother over the years. She needed to stick around and ride herd on Tony, to make sure those samples arrived in each and every store.

"Sure." Rick gave her a deeply disappointed look.

She sent him a mutinous glare. "Rick—"

He loosened his tie as if it were choking him, keeping his eyes on her face all the while. He challenged mildly, "Chicken to be alone with me, huh?"

"I am not chicken!"

"Then why not go with me?" he asked.

She stalked back to her desk and stared down at the million and one things she had to do. "Because I'm busy."

He thrust his hands into his pockets again and leaned back against the glass, his legs crossed at the ankles, his body at a slant. "Oh, really."

"I am!" She whirled on him emotionally. "I have all my notes to go over for my interview with the *Wall Street Journal* tomorrow afternoon."

"So review your notes in the morning," Rick urged flatly. "It's almost five."

"Three on the West Coast," Caroline corrected, unwilling to admit to herself how tempted she was simply to give in to him and to her own desire to be with him.

"And six on the East. Our time is what counts, Caroline. Come on," he urged, his eyes suddenly as soft and persuasive as his voice. "One night. What could it hurt to leave the office on time? Unless of course you think the board is so dissatisfied with your performance as an executive that they're just waiting for an excuse to dump you."

Caroline bristled. "I have every right to leave at five or six with everyone else."

"Now you're talking." Rick closed the distance between them swiftly, grabbed her purse with one hand, her elbow with his other and hustled her out the door.

Caroline could have fought him, but she didn't. It had been a long week. She was tired. The next two days were going to be very difficult, too. She needed a break. Taking the time to revitalize herself could only be good for the business long-term, she assured herself firmly.

"Rick—?" Caroline dragged her feet as they approached the elevators.

"What?" His voice was soft, warm and soothing against her ear. He turned her to face him.

"Your wife, Susan." Caroline paused and wet her lips. "Was she really a workaholic?"

"Yes," he said grimly. "She really was."

"YOU KNOW THAT home-cooked meal you owe me for accompanying you to the engagement party your mother threw for us?" Rick drawled, a scant two hours later as the two of them sat on the wooden deck of his beach house that overlooked the Gulf. They had changed into shorts and T-shirts and sweat socks as soon as they had arrived. And though Rick's clothes were a little large on her, Caroline was enjoying the glorious February day. They didn't have many days like this in Houston. Comfortably warm and sunny, but not humid.

"Yeah, what about it?" she finally asked.

"Well, forget it," Rick said genially. "I'll settle for just spending time with you. You can count tonight as payback."

Caroline turned to him suspiciously. It wasn't like Rick to accept less than was due him. "Why?" she asked warily.

"Isn't it obvious?" Rick chuckled with affection as he looked down at the long-handled barbecue fork in her hand. "You might be the prettiest woman this side of the Mississippi, but you can't cook."

Caroline's mouth dropped open. "I can, too, cook!"

Rick chuckled and shook his head in bemusement. "I beg to differ with you there, princess," he drawled.

"Now hold on just a minute. You have no idea how I cook," Caroline accused.

He raised a dissenting brow. "You're burning the hell out of that hot dog."

Caroline looked down at the blackened edges on the meat. "I'll have you know I like my hot dogs blackened, just like I like my redfish."

"Blackened or charred beyond all recognition?" Rick probed with an insolent grin.

Deciding her hot dog was done, Caroline took it off the grill and spread generous dollops of mustard across the steaming frankfurter and squishy soft white bun. "You don't know what you're missing."

Watching her lick the excess mustard from her fingers, Rick thought he did...the sweet touch of her tongue dueling with his and the soft yielding pressure of her lips.

He also knew she was a workaholic, just like his wife had been. The difference there was Caroline showed promising signs of change. Her coming to the beach with him tonight, for instance, meant she could switch priorities, if pressed. And he intended to press her a lot from now on.

"What are you thinking about?" Caroline asked.

You, he thought. But he couldn't tell her that. Ignoring the pressure in his groin, Rick turned his attention back to the grill. He studied his hot dog.

Maybe he'd better keep his mind on cooking for both their sakes, instead of the way his old T-shirt softly molded her breasts and how his loose beach shorts hiked up on her slim thighs.

"Take a good look, Caroline," he finally said. "This is a hot dog that's been grilled to perfection."

She frowned. "Looks half-done to me."

Rick squinted at her. "Where'd you ever learn to cook anyway?"

"I didn't," she admitted with a flirtatious toss of her long dark hair. "If I had, though, it would've been from my mother."

"Marjorie can cook?" Rick was truly amazed.

Caroline sighed. "Mother can do everything that pleases a man."

And so, Rick thought, Caroline, obstinate as ever, took the opposite tact. For several moments they just drifted along, content just to be with each other.

"Rick?" Caroline asked softly at last, a peculiarly tentative note in her low voice.

"Hmm?" Rick tore his gaze from the spectacular sunset, turned his eyes to her face and found it infinitely more beautiful, infinitely more compelling.

"Why didn't you ever tell me before today that you had been married?"

He shrugged. "How come you never asked?"

"Because I just assumed you hadn't been," she explained, tucking a stray lock of hair behind one delicate ear.

"Why did you think that?"

"Because you seem like a ladies' man."

"Am I now?" he drawled.

"You know what I mean," she corrected with a reproving lift of her slender brow. "You charm everyone. The owner of the catering service, my mother." *Me.*

"Just because I enjoy the company of women, doesn't mean I'm shallow," Rick said. His eyes met and held hers. "If and when I get married again, Caroline, that'll be it."

"You're serious," she said slowly, looking simultaneously stunned and pleased at his revelation. Shy color lit her cheeks. Her silver earrings, shaped like the state of Texas, swung softly in the breeze.

"Very serious." Rick paused. "The question is, what kind of man do you want, princess? One who's all business—like Hugh?"

Her pretty eyes gleamed with a sexy, speculative light. "Or more fun than a barrel of monkeys, like you."

He grinned, liking the way her smile lit up her hazel eyes. "Now you're teasing me."

"Maybe."

"Why?"

Finished with her hot dog and diet soda, Caroline discarded her napkin, got up restlessly and paced back and forth. "Because all this serious talk unnerves me." *It makes me feel like we're really engaged.*

Rick smiled. "Why?"

The late-afternoon sun had left a blush on his cheeks and nose. His black hair was windblown, his look both intent and mischievous. She swallowed hard, knowing if she didn't keep a handle on things, no one would. "Because this evening is starting to feel too romantic," she said.

Rick's sexy grin widened. "Too romantic? I didn't know there was any such thing."

Heart racing, she watched him approach. "Well, there is." She stood with her back to a rail.

He stopped just beside her. "You still don't trust me, do you?"

I want to, Caroline thought. She studied the toe of one of the oversize sweat socks on her feet. "I don't trust romance, Rick. There's a difference."

He backed against the rail, too. "But why not?"

"Because . . . you know I made a complete and utter fool of myself once, when I thought I was in love. And my mother's got an amazing lack of judgment in that area, and we share the same genes.

I don't want to become as hormone-driven and ir-rational as my mother, Rick." *I don't want to be hurt.*

Rick circled around in front of her, put his hands on her shoulders and let them slide halfway down her arms, where they continued to cup her warmly. "Sweetheart, the two of you couldn't be more dif-ferent," he said softly. "Your mother, bless her heart, is as flighty as the day is long. Whereas you are rock steady and clear thinking."

"Then why is it when I'm with you that I feel like I'm walking on air?" Caroline whispered misera-bly. Why did her life take on a fairy-tale quality whenever she was with him?

Rick's arms slid around her back. He drew her close, so they were touching in one long electrified line. "Because what we have is real and solid and enduring," he said gruffly. Framing her face with his hands, he forced her gaze up to his. "Trust me, Caroline," he implored in a soft, urgent voice. "Trust in this." He lowered his head and took her mouth in a searing kiss.

It felt so good to be wanted and touched. It felt so good to be held against him. Desire trembled in-side her, making her insides go all soft and syrupy. Her legs trembled. Her hips moved. How could this be wrong when he made her feel so loved and cher-ished. She melted helplessly against him, thigh to thigh, sex to sex. Business didn't come into this. And as far as greed, the only greed they had was for each other.

Her heart was thudding heavily in her chest. She opened her mouth and coaxed his tongue outward. He tasted so good, so undeniably male. Needing to be closer, she stood on tiptoe and wrapped one arm about his shoulders. She used the other hand to sift through the dark windblown strands of his hair. Over and over she stroked the thick, silky strands, until he moaned. He anchored an arm about her waist, lifted her easily off her feet and walked her to the side of the house.

Sheltered by the overhang of the roof and the shimmering darkness, the wall to her back, he pressed against her. The thin shorts they wore were no protection. She could feel his erection pressing against her, hot and urgent. His forearms moved to either side of her and lay flat against the wall. The warm hard pressure of his body effectively trapped her into place. They kissed languidly at first, then with growing passion. His hand cupped her breast and slipped beneath the hem of her T-shirt. She had taken off her bra along with her business suit and he had no trouble locating the roundness of her breasts. Her gasp of delight echoed in the stillness of the air as he rubbed first one peak, then the other, into tight rosy buds.

He looked down at her. When their glances meshed, she could see the fever in his gaze, the tenderness, the love. . . .

"I stopped the other day," he reminded her on a brusque, uneven note.

"To our mutual regret."

He released a trembling breath and his voice dropped another rough note. "You're not making it easy on me, princess."

She drew in a trembling breath. "I don't want to make it easy for you, Rick."

He gave her a sexy half smile and teased, "You want to make it hard for me? Is that it?"

"What I want," she said slowly, as her hand shyly went to the hard ridge of arousal in his pants, and ran along its edge, "is for you to be aching in as many places as I already am."

His hand closed over hers, holding her against him. "That you've already got, princess. That you've already got."

She felt herself grow a little dizzier and a little wilder. It was as if there was a new, more sensual woman inside her Rick was helping her to discover.

He groaned as her hand trailed across his stomach to slip beneath the hem of his T-shirt and caress his chest. "If we start this," he warned, on a shudder, bending slightly and pressing a tiny string of hot wet kisses down the nape of her neck, "there's no turning back...."

"I don't want to turn back," she whispered. *I'm sure of my feelings for you. Sure of your love for me.*

His legs pinning hers to the wall, he bent his head and kissed her again. Only there was no question this time about what he wanted or what was coming next. Only passion so hot it sizzled. His tongue swept along hers, circled it and flicked across the edges of her teeth, before dipping deep. Breathlessly, she responded. He groaned as her teeth closed around his tongue, then he took control again, scoring the inside of her mouth in a rhythm of penetration and retreat. He paused to yank off his T-shirt. It landed next to them on one of the chaises. She stared at the splendor of his male physique. He was perfect. So hard and solid all over. Her mouth went dry.

"You next, princess."

Before she could do more than gasp, he'd divested her of her shirt. He looked down at her breasts, his gaze lovingly roving every inch. "No bra," he whispered. He touched one taut, straining peak and gently laved it with his tongue. The electricity of his touch made her shudder. "Why?" he asked huskily.

"The underwire was bothering me."

"Bull." He grinned with boyish appeal. "You wanted me to be able to see the imprint of your nipples against your shirt. You wanted me aching all night, unable to think about anything but touching you like this." He rubbed his hands across her nipples until she sucked in her breath. "And this." He covered her breasts with both palms and massaged them fully until she trembled. "And this." He fit his lips around the tip of her breast and suckled lightly, until she strained against him. Wanting more. Wanting everything.

"So what if I did, Rick?" She threaded her hands through his hair, holding him close, wanting his slow, sensual possession of her never to stop.

"So nothing." He came back up to kiss her thoroughly, taking her mouth in a slow mating dance. "I liked it," he whispered against her hot, waiting mouth. "I like you. And now—"

"Now what?" she asked breathlessly as he slowly rubbed his chest across her bared breasts, tantalizing her budding nipples with the silky mat of his chest hair and the hard muscle beneath.

"Now, you get your reward for teasing me until I was half out of my mind with wanting you," he promised softly, skimming the curves and valleys of her bared breasts, rubbing his fingertips across her nipples, until she was quaking with sensations she could hardly bear. She moved her hips, rubbing against him, into him, until he was shuddering, too. She was so empty inside. So tired of being without him.

"Oh, Rick," Caroline whispered. Sensual lightning swept through her, making even the few clothes she wore an unbearable nuisance. "I want to touch you," she whispered. She slid her hands from his sides, to the small of his spine, learning anew the sleek male contours of his hips and buttocks and thighs. As she drew the shorts down, past his thighs, she elicited a low groan from his lips. His whole body was quaking. He stepped out of his shorts and underwear and kicked them away.

"Now you," he said, his eyes holding hers, as her breath caught.

He disrobed her slowly, first loosening the drawstring that held the shorts up, then pushing them down below her knees. Caroline was so aroused, she could barely breathe.

"I want you," she whispered.

"I know." He stayed her hand before she could remove the tiny scrap of damp lace panties, too. He stepped toward her, not stopping until the hard length of his arousal pressed between her legs. She trembled from the fit of his body against hers, from the pressure nudging her feminine cleft, from the frustration of not yet being skin to skin. Again he bent to kiss her. As his hands searched out the contours of her breasts, she rocked against him, moving back and forth, up and down, over and back and across. Wildfire swept through her, making her moan.

He caught her limp body and held it against him until the quaking inside her had stopped. The next thing she knew the panties were off. He stepped between her legs, nudging her legs apart. She opened herself up to him as gently and irrevocably as a flower blooms in the spring. He caught her by the hips to steady her, and then they were one. Beautifully so.

"I don't want to rush," he said.

"Neither do I." Caroline rocked against him gently, even though holding back was torture.

"Am I hurting you?" He trembled with the need to hold back his own release as he loved her an inch at a time, going deeper and deeper.

"No...harder, Rick...." she demanded. Her composure was gone and his would soon be, too.

"Like this?" Rick asked, delving slowly.

"Yes," she whispered, rocking against him, closing tight. "Just like this—oh, Rick" *I love you so much!*

"Yes, Princess. That's it. Say my name. Say it over and over again." He kissed her again voraciously, satisfying one hunger and feeding another. "Let me know I'm the one you want."

"I do—I want you to love me." *Just as I love you.*

He pinned her to the wall with his hips. He pressed into her as deeply as he could go, then withdrew. And then he filled her again. Over and over again he moved, taking her until both of them were straining, gasping, lost in the pleasure and one another...until he was so deeply buried in her that they were one, free-falling into ecstasy.

"I HAVE A BED in there, you know," Rick drawled lazily, long moments later. He was unable to remember when he had ever felt so happy.

"I know." Caroline sighed contentedly.

"We could move," he suggested, though he'd hate to. She felt so good against him.

"No." Caroline cuddled closer, draping one smooth sexy leg between his hair-roughened ones.

She loved the way their naked bodies fit together beneath the thick fluffy beach towel. "I like it here, on the chaise."

Rick's arm curved a little tighter around her bare shoulders. "It is nice, isn't it?" he remarked, unable to think when he'd ever felt so at peace. "Listening to the ocean. Looking up at the stars overhead."

She traced patterns through the whirling hair on his chest. "Nicer still to be here with you."

"Why, Caroline Lord," Rick drawled, exaggerating every syllable to comic effect, "was that a *romantic* thought you just expressed?"

She aimed a playful fist at the thick mat of hair on his chest. "Cut it out."

Ignoring her admonishment, he tweaked her nose. "It was, wasn't it?" he prodded.

"Yes, it was," she said. "You've changed me."

He studied her, thinking about how much he'd come to like seeing her in the weeks they'd been engaged. "You've changed me, too," he admitted gently, as he combed his fingers through her hair.

Caroline shifted her weight and rolled gracefully onto her stomach. She propped her chin on her fist. "How so?"

Rick shrugged. "I've seen my sisters get married, one by one, and while I envied them their families, I didn't think I'd ever want to settle down again. And certainly not with a woman who was devoted to her work. Yet women who didn't have exciting, challenging careers didn't interest me. Somehow, it was easier just to keep moving on. But I can see now that's not the way to go at all."

"Oh, really?"

He rubbed a hand up and down her spine. "Being alone doesn't begin to square with this."

Her eyes sparkled. "I'm glad to hear that, because after tonight you definitely couldn't go back to that."

"I wouldn't want to," Rick said seriously. "The fact of the matter is—" his voice caught emotionally "—I could love you every night the rest of my life and never grow tired of the sight of you."

"I know what you mean," she whispered, happy tears filling her eyes. "I feel that way, too."

The only thing that still bothered Rick about Caroline was her single-minded devotion to her career. But hadn't she proven she'd changed by leaving her office on a moment's notice and coming here with him tonight?

She curled against him contentedly, the silence between them broken only by the growl of her stomach.

"Don't tell me you're hungry again," he teased.

"For you, always."

He grinned down at her. He fully intended to make love to her again. But first he would see to her other appetites. "That reminds me," he drawled. "We never did get around to eating our dessert."

"That's right, we didn't, did we?"

"Wait here."

He returned with his terry-cloth robe for her and an armful of goodies. While she shrugged into the robe, he wrapped the beach towel they'd had drawn over them around his waist. He knew she didn't mind his nakedness; he also knew there was no sense tempting fate. It was going to be hard enough getting all the way through dessert without kissing her again.

Caroline padded barefoot over to the grill, to examine the white-hot coals. "I haven't had s'mores since I was a kid," she confessed as she poked two fat marshmallows onto the end of a long-handled cooking fork.

Rick wished her derriere didn't curve quite so enticingly, even when wrapped in his overly large robe. "Well, not to worry," he assured her, tearing his eyes from the slim pair of legs peeking out from beneath the hem of the robe. "I've got plenty of graham crackers and a whole package of Hershey's bars."

Caroline made a regretful face. "You shouldn't have told me that."

"Insatiable, hmm?"

Her eyes locked with his and held. "Very."

They went back to toasting marshmallows. Rick glanced at his, saw it was golden brown on both sides. Caroline was blackening hers deliberately. "I should've known," Rick lamented, shaking his head.

She grinned at him playfully. "Should've known what?"

"That you'd scorch the hell out of your marshmallows, too."

She looked askance at the marshmallow he'd layered between two graham crackers and half a Hershey's bar. She leaned back in her deck chair and crossed her legs at the knee. "If you're not going to roast your marshmallows until they're nice and crunchy, what's the point of cooking them over an open fire? We could just as soon *melt* them down in the microwave."

"Now there's a thought," he drawled, aware it'd only been a matter of minutes since they'd last made love. He let his glance trail up over her slowly, from the exposed line of one luscious thigh where her robe parted at the knee, to her slim waist, and full breasts. His hot glance bypassed her bow-shaped lips to her eyes. "It'd be a heck of a lot faster," he finally said.

"Ah, yes," she admitted, stopping to blow on the flaming marshmallow. "But not nearly as pleasurable."

"True." His pulse accelerating, he watched her assemble the layers of her own s'more. "Want to know something?"

"What?" Caroline asked between mouthfuls of the gooey treat.

"I have never enjoyed being with a woman more than I enjoyed being with you tonight."

She nudged him with her bare foot. "You're kind of fun yourself, fella." She rolled her napkin into a ball, turned and shot it into the wastebasket next to the door.

"Just kind of?" he taunted in a low, desire-packed voice.

"Well…" Caroline rested an index finger against her chin and pretended to think about it.

"Reserving judgment until after round two?" Rick crossed the distance between them swiftly and pulled her into his arms.

Caroline laced her arms around his neck. "Is there going to be a round two?" she asked.

"As well as three and four," Rick affirmed, knowing he could easily make love to her the whole night through and never tire. Deciding enough time had been wasted, he dropped his towel to the deck and kissed her thoroughly, tasting the rich blend of melted chocolate, toasted marshmallow, graham cracker and Caroline. Nothing had ever been so sweet.

The sight and feel of his nakedness inflamed her already aroused senses. Needing no further encouragement, Caroline parted the edges of her borrowed robe and drew him close. At the touch of his skin to hers, every inch of her tingled. She looked up into his face, wishing they could stay this way forever, intimately locked in each other's arms.

She wished they could remain on this deserted stretch of Texas beach. "I love you, Rick," she said softly. *There, she had said it. And meant it with all her heart.*

He looked deep into her eyes and squeezed her tightly. "I love you, too."

Chapter Ten

"Well, finally!" Tony yelled the moment a groggy Rick handed her the phone.

Every muscle in her body was fluid and relaxed. Caroline yawned and glanced through the bedroom window. The first pale yellow light of dawn was streaming in through the linen curtains. A glance at the digital clock on the bedside table confirmed it was as early as she thought, only 6:14. She moaned, realizing she'd only had a couple hours' sleep, if that. She glanced at Rick. They exchanged smiles. He wordlessly linked fingers with her.

"I've been looking for you all night!" Tony continued.

Caroline wished she could slide into Rick's arms and go back to sleep. "How'd you find me?" she asked her brother groggily.

"It wasn't easy," Tony grumbled. "And why didn't you call me back yesterday? Didn't you get any of my messages? I left five!"

"No. I didn't." And that was strange, because Sue Ellen was very efficient. "What's going on, Tony?"

"You remember those shaving-cream samples for the bonus gift packs?"

"Yes."

"Well, they didn't arrive yesterday."

Caroline sat bolt upright. Her shoulders were rigid with tension. "What do you mean they didn't arrive?"

"Exactly what I said. I started getting calls late yesterday afternoon from stores around the country. Everyone was expecting them. Instead, everyone got bottles of Stolen Moments perfume."

"So where is the shaving cream?"

"That's what I'm asking you!"

"You're the vice president in charge of shipping!"

"Look, I gave the right orders. It's just . . . there was a screwup somewhere."

"Have you been able to track it down?"

"Nope. Not yet. The plant manager in Kansas swears the shipments all went out on time—"

"How does he explain the perfume?"

"He doesn't."

"What do you mean?"

"He says they boxed up the right samples, that the distribution center must've screwed up. The distribution center manager says they simply labeled what the manufacturing plant sent to them."

Caroline could feel a massive tension headache coming on. "So where are the samples of shaving cream?"

"That's just it, no one knows. They tore the Kansas City warehouse apart last night. No samples were found. So meanwhile, sister dear, we have every store across the country on our backs because they have received every other part of the bonus gift for men!"

"So now we've got ads and photo displays, but no product!"

"That about sums it up, yes."

Caroline swore heatedly. This new men's line and "Max," the fragrance that was part of it, was supposed to be a testament to her father. It was also the last product he had created before he died. If he could see them now, he'd think, as no doubt did everyone else, that his faith in her ability to run the company had been misplaced.

"So what do we do now?" Tony demanded.

Caroline threw the sheet back and climbed out of bed. Carrying the portable phone in one hand, she began to gather up her clothes. "We fix it. Just sit tight, Tony. I'll be right there."

"When?"

She frowned. "I don't know. Maybe forty-five minutes, if traffic isn't too bad. As soon as I can." She put the antenna down and tossed the portable phone to Rick. He replaced it on the stand.

All too aware of his eyes upon her, Caroline began to dress. She frowned at the run in her stocking and wished she had another pair with her, but she didn't.

Rick swung his legs over the edge of the bed and rubbed the sleep from his eyes. "What's going on?"

Caroline shook her head, too upset to go over it blow by blow. "Nothing."

"Nothing?" His brows lifted in disbelief. "You leap out of bed like a woman possessed and I'm expected to believe it's nothing?"

She didn't have time for this. She hadn't had time for last night. "There's a problem at the office," Caroline snapped. "The whole company is going to have egg on its face if I don't fix it." She would lose the presidency, let down her father and destroy her life all in one fell swoop. It couldn't get more disastrous than that.

Rick got up hurriedly. His expression was as grave as hers. "If you want to use my phone to start tracking the shipments—"

"Thanks, but no." Caroline cut off his offer brusquely. Ignoring the hurt she saw in his eyes, she continued, "All my files are at the office. Plus I have that meeting with the *Wall Street Journal* reporter. If I don't talk to him, he's bound to figure out something's very wrong."

Rick gathered his clothes and headed for the adjacent bathroom. "Give me a second and I'll drive you in."

Caroline thought about arguing with him, then decided it would only waste more time. "Hurry."

"I will."

Rick did hurry, but when he came out of the bathroom, she was gone. So was his car. So were his keys.

"THANKS FOR LEAVING me stranded," Rick began curtly, several hours later.

She looked up from her desk. Somewhere in the time that had ensued, she had managed to shower and put on a fresh set of clothes—a trim two-piece suit that buttoned all the way to her throat. She hadn't put on any makeup yet and her hair was still damp.

"I left you cab fare," Caroline said.

"And that makes it all right to steal my car?" Why couldn't she have waited the minute it had taken him to put his pants and shirt on?

Caroline shrugged and reached for the phone. "I assumed you wouldn't mind."

He covered her hand, hating the ice-cold look in her hazel eyes. She was acting as if nothing had happened between them last night.

Caroline shut her eyes. "Rick, please, I'm in the middle of a crisis here."

"More than one kind," he agreed in a gruff tone that brought her head up. "I thought we meant something to each other. I thought we *trusted* each other, Caroline."

She swallowed and turned even paler. Removing her hand from beneath his, she pushed away from the desk and rose. "And I thought you understood just how much it means to me to run the company my father started. I've worked for this for so long."

Rick knew all about dreams. He also knew about love. What he and Caroline had shared was more important to him than any business deal, but she obviously didn't feel the same. "Fine," he said brusquely. "If that's the way you want it, Caroline, I'm out of here." He pivoted on his heel and headed for the door.

"Fine." She whisked him away with a wave of her hands. "Go."

He turned and surveyed her coldly. She was a stranger to him this morning. Nothing like the warm, loving woman who had shared his bed with him last night. But maybe, Rick thought, he had only been seeing what he wanted to see. Maybe he'd been deluding himself. "You really have a heart of steel, you know that?"

To his surprise, Caroline stormed over to close the door and prevent him from leaving. "What is it you don't understand, Rick? The fact I have a business to run? Or the fact that I am ticked off at you for last night!"

"What do you mean you're mad at me?" he exclaimed in astonishment.

She leaned against the door, blocking his exit. "You heard me."

"Heard you, maybe. But I don't understand." He stepped nearer, searching her upturned face. "Why would you be mad about last night?" When she didn't respond, he leaned in closer, bracing a hand on either side of her. "Didn't I satisfy you last night, Caroline?" he asked softly.

Caroline turned her head away from him stubbornly. "Stop it." She shoved the words out from behind a row of white teeth.

"Or were those cries I heard, cries of shame and not ecstasy—"

Caroline swung her head back to face him. Her eyes glittered. "I told you to stop it," she said.

"Why? Because it makes you uncomfortable to remember what a passionate woman you are?"

"I'm not—I'm not like that." She placed a hand on the middle of his chest and shoved. Rick stayed where he was.

She dropped her hand in silent fury and started to duck beneath his outstretched arm. He dropped his arm slightly, and refused to let her go.

"Yes, you are, Caroline. You're a passionate person. We both are, and there's nothing wrong with that."

"You just don't get it, do you?" Her chin lifted another notch. "I had responsibilities here, Rick. And you talked me into leaving them. If I had been here, or even left word where I was going, Tony would've been able to get in touch with me hours ago. I could have tracked down those lost samples last night. And the crisis would have been fixed by now, instead of just half fixed."

"Right," he pointed out impatiently. "Your business problem would have been fixed Caroline. But you and I would never have had last night...or have said we loved each other."

Caroline walked away from him and back to her seat behind the desk. "Rick, we could've done that anytime,'' she said. "But the launch for the men's line is tomorrow!''

Rick studied her, not sure when he had ever felt so disappointed in someone. "First things first, I guess,'' he decided grimly.

"This is *business,* Rick.''

His fury mounting, Rick strode closer. He leaned across her desk, his palms braced on either side of her, and lowered his face until they were at eye level with one another. "And what's our love affair, Caroline?'' he asked softly. "Inconsequential?''

She flinched but didn't back down. "In the face of the millions we stand to lose, yes!'' Caroline shouted.

Rick was silent a long moment. "So why didn't you let me help you?'' he asked. "Why did you just run out on me this morning?''

For a second, Caroline looked as miserable as he felt. "Because it was my problem,'' she whispered.

Rick sighed, cleared a space and sat on the edge of her desk. "People who are in love with one another share their problems, Caroline. But that's not on your agenda, is it? You won't ever allow yourself to loosen up or change or really believe that there is anything more in life than your family business!''

"I have a responsibility here, Rick!'' she exclaimed.

His jaw tightened. "To Maxwell Lord but not to me."

Caroline didn't so much as blink. "My responsibility to Maxwell Lord comes first, yes."

He had lived that way once. Not again. "I guess I know where I stand." He turned and headed for the door. Once again, Caroline vaulted to her feet and beat him to the exit.

"Wait a minute, Rick." She clamped a soft, feminine hand on his arm. He stopped but didn't look at her. In the tense silence that fell, he thought he heard her swallow.

"Aren't you going to escort me to the launch party for Maxwell Lord for Men?"

Fighting to control his soaring temper, Rick closed his eyes. *Business.* He shrugged free of her light, acquiescing grasp. "Take yourself."

"HOW COULD YOU DO THIS to me?" Caroline demanded angrily thirty-six hours later. "How could you do this to Maxwell Lord?"

"Call it a reality check," Hugh Bradford retorted unapologetically to both Caroline and Tony. He looked at Caroline. "The job of company president is a demanding one. I wanted to see how you would handle a crisis."

"At the expense of Maxwell Lord's reputation?" Caroline questioned coldly.

"There was never any real danger of the company's reputation being impugned. I would've had the samples delivered in time, even if you hadn't tracked them down so efficiently. The public never would've known there was anything amiss. So no harm was done," Hugh explained.

"The hell there wasn't," Tony said gruffly. "Your shenanigans put Caroline and me through the wringer."

Hugh didn't dispute that. He had watched over every agonizing moment of the crisis, from afar. He thrust both hands into the pockets of his expensive suit pants. "How'd you find out it was me?"

"Easy," Tony said.

Caroline continued, "You were the only one with something to gain by making Tony and I both look bad with the board. I want your resignation, Hugh. Effective immediately."

Hugh tossed her his electronic badge. "Fine. It's your loss. I was going to resign if I wasn't made president, anyway." He turned and sauntered out. The door slammed behind him.

Caroline stared after him, wondering how she ever could have dated the man. Had she really been that blind? Or had Hugh just been good at covering up his treacherous, back-stabbing soul?

"Cheer up, Caroline," Tony said, laying a comforting hand on her shoulder. "Hugh's right, much as I hate to admit it. His dirty trick did some good. The crisis brought the two of us back together and showed us how well we work as a team, when we give it half a try. And it also showed me I have no wish to shoulder the burden of president."

"You mean that, don't you?" Caroline studied his face.

Tony nodded. "Besides, you deserve the job. After all, you're the one who found the warehouse where all the shaving cream had erroneously been sent.

"Not to mention the fact that we've hit record sales on both coasts, as well as in the heartland and the south." Tony handed her the computer printouts that had just come in via electronic mail. "Thanks to your expert handling, Caroline, Maxwell Lord for Men is a smashing success. Of course, sales might have been helped by timing the launch for Valentine's Day."

"I'm sure they were," Caroline said sadly, recalling that, too, had been her idea.

"So why so glum?" Tony looked at his watch. "I know technically, since it's 11:49 p.m., that Valentine's Day is almost over, but you've still got time to celebrate. And after the crisis we've weathered, you deserve to. Just call Rick and—"

"No. I can't. I'm . . . exhausted from the launch party last night."

Tony frowned. "How come Rick wasn't there?"

"He had other commitments," Caroline said shortly.

"Is that why you're unhappy?" Tony said gently. "Because Rick wasn't at the launch party?"

Caroline said nothing.

"I'd think today of all days it would be especially important for him to show up with some candy or flowers or something," Tony said.

Caroline thought so, too, but said flatly, "If I'm still upset, and I admit I am, it's because the fiasco with the lost shaving cream should never have happened. It was an expensive mistake."

"But you handled it like a pro. The board was impressed. Enough to vote you in as president a whole week early. Aren't you happy about that?" Tony pressed.

Happy? How could she be happy when Rick wasn't speaking to her? Knowing how romantic he was, that it was indeed Valentine's Day, she had half expected him to come waltzing in with an apology and a bouquet of flowers or something, but he hadn't. And his continued silence was more telling than she wanted to admit. He had been serious yesterday. It was over between them.

"Is Rick coming to the party Mother's throwing to celebrate your election as permanent president tomorrow night?"

"I don't know," Caroline answered evasively, wishing she could assure her brother that Rick would show up but knowing better than to count on Rick for anything except more grief about what he called her workaholic attitudes. She picked up her suit jacket and shrugged it on. "I left a message on his machine."

Tony walked her to the door. "And?"

"And I haven't heard from him," Caroline said sadly.

"STILL TROUBLE in paradise?" Tony prodded Caroline the following evening when eight o'clock passed, and then nine o'clock, and ten, and Rick still hadn't shown up.

Caroline clutched the champagne glass in her hand.

"Why don't you just admit to one and all that you made a mistake getting engaged so quickly? I mean, now that you have the presidency, what's the point in continuing something that's obviously not working for either of you?"

"That's a good question," a low male voice interrupted. "But not one Caroline's at liberty to answer at the moment. Hello, princess." Rick bent down to give her a cursory peck on the brow. It was a quick, casual caress, but there was no warmth in it. No feeling. Caroline's heart sank. He may be saying all the right things, but he's touching me like a stranger, she thought.

"Rick." To her annoyance, her voice was a little breathy and altogether too relieved.

"Tony, if you'll excuse us?" Rick slid his hand beneath her elbow and drew her away. He kept walking until they reached the French doors at the other end of the room.

"You made it."

Rick shrugged. His eyes, when they touched hers, were remote. "Did you think I wouldn't?"

Caroline looked down at the untouched drink in her hand. "I didn't know."

"I guess you got your business crisis resolved."

She nodded. Her stomach fluttered with a thousand butterflies. "Yes." *Tell me we can work this out,* she pleaded silently.

"As well as everything else you wanted," Rick continued.

But surely, she thought, he'll realize our lives can only get easier now. "Who told you?"

"Marjorie." Rick lifted a glass from a tray and drank deeply of the brandy. His voice was so casual, it stung. "She said the board took an early vote so they could time the announcement with the *Wall Street Journal* interview that's going to be out tomorrow morning."

"Yes." Caroline nodded. "That was nice."

"So you finally got what you wanted." He finished his brandy in a single draught.

I don't have you. "So did you," she said.

Rick flinched. "Yeah, the spa deal came through—true."

Silence fell between them, even more awkward now.

"So, now that we're both as happy as two bears with a honey pot," Rick said sarcastically, "when do you want to tell your mother the wedding is off?"

"Delayed," Caroline corrected quickly.

"All right. Delayed," Rick agreed brusquely. "So when do you want to tell her?"

His curt tone rattled her even more than the aloof contempt in his gaze. Drawing what was left of her pride around her like an invisible force field, Caroline said stiffly, "I don't know. Maybe Saturday."

"Why wait?" Rick's jaw took on an aggressive edge. "Why not make it tonight?"

Caroline let out an exasperated breath. She should have known Rick would be difficult. "What's the rush?" she demanded, mocking his tone.

"I'll tell you what the rush is." He leaned close enough to whisper in her ear. "I'm tired of playing this charade, Caroline. And frankly, I'd think you would be, too." He straightened and gave her a direct look.

It's no charade, Rick, she wanted to say. "I'm sorry about the way I ran out on you."

"Are you?"

The unchecked sarcasm in his voice stung.

"Then tell me this, Caroline. If the same thing happened again, would you do anything differently?"

"In the same situation?"

"*Yes!*"

"No," she said.

"That's what I thought." He looked at her as if she had just sealed the lid on her own coffin. He pressed a light cursory kiss to her brow. "Well, now that I've made my appearance, I think I'll be going."

And then he was gone.

"SO ALL THIS TIME the two of you were pulling my leg with the engagement?" Marjorie asked, later that same night.

Caroline curled up beside her mother on the sofa. "Yes. It was a lousy trick. It's made us all miserable."

"I'm not. It allowed you to meet Rick."

"Another story," Caroline murmured, getting up to pace the room restlessly.

"What, dear?"

"I said that's another story." *One I have no wish to go into! If only I could stop thinking about him, stop wanting him.*

"Aha, so the two of you did have a falling-out," Marjorie said presumptuously, with all the excitement of a television journalist on the trail of a hot story.

"He wants to end the pretense, now that we've both got everything we want."

"And how do you feel?"

I'll miss seeing him. "I want him to be happy," Caroline said.

"And what will it take to make him happy?" Marjorie asked.

Caroline let out an exasperated sigh. "He wants a devoted wife. You know, the kind who stays home and cooks all the time and fetches his paper and slippers." The kind who didn't burn the hot dogs and marshmallows and didn't give a damn about her work.

Marjorie frowned. "That doesn't sound like the Rick I know."

"Believe it. Why do you think he's never married again?"

Marjorie did a double take. "Again?"

"Another long story."

Her mother studied her. Her expression gentled, then turned to one of understanding, mixed with pity. "You love him, don't you, darling?" she asked softly.

"Love?" Caroline echoed. "Who knows? What is love, anyway?"

"Only the most magical feeling in the whole world," Marjorie said with her customary theatrical flair.

Caroline tucked her knees under her chin, and wrapped her arms around her legs. "Unfortunately, that feeling goes away, and when it does, you're left more alone than ever."

"I was hoping it would be better for you than it has been for me," Marjorie said, looking as distressed as Caroline felt.

Unfortunately, Caroline thought, it wasn't. And realizing that made her feel as if her heart would break.

Chapter Eleven

"You know, I thought you'd be deliriously happy since Mom has gone back to Los Angeles," Tony said, as he joined Caroline in her office.

Caroline put down the sales reports for the new men's line—it was still breaking records, two weeks after the launch—and looked at her brother. "You know, it's funny. She's always annoyed me so much, mostly because she meddles in my life whenever she is around. But now that she's gone again—" Caroline paused "—I miss her."

"Me, too." Tony was quiet.

"Never fear." Caroline got up and went to the small refrigerator in the corner and took out two individual cans of diet soda. "She's coming back, as soon as her miniseries has finished filming. She's going to work on your love life next."

Tony groaned and took the can Caroline passed him. "I thought she would've given up after she failed at trying to fix yours. Sorry.'' He held up a hand before she could voice her protest. ''I didn't mean to insult you.''

''I know.'' Caroline sighed and sank down into her chair. She popped open her can of soda. ''Besides, what you said is true—my love life is as much of a wreck as ever.''

Tony studied her face. ''So, you're still pining for Rick, aren't you, Caroline?''

'' 'Pining'!'' she echoed, incensed. Feeling more restless than ever, she got out of her chair and took a stack of papers that didn't need to be filed to the file cabinet. ''What an old-fashioned word.''

Tony watched her stuff the papers in the front of the drawer, before the alphabetized dividers. ''Love is an old-fashioned feeling, or so I've been told.''

''Unfortunately, it doesn't last.'' Caroline slammed the file drawer then marched back to her seat and dropped into it. Making no effort to hide her aggravation with her brother, she said, ''Look at Dad and Mother.''

''Look at Ozzie and Harriet,'' Tony countered, listing a marriage that had lasted.

Caroline volleyed back with one that had ended. ''Lucy and Ricky.''

''Paul Newman and Joanne Woodward. And you, dear sister, have always worn your heart on your sleeve.'' Tony gave her a direct look. ''You're in love with Rick. And whether he likes it or not, Rick is in love with you."

"Whoa." Caroline held up a palm in front of her. "Hold it right there. Rick does not love me."

"How did you come to that conclusion?" Tony asked.

"Because he walked out on me at the first available opportunity."

"Was this before or after you walked out on him?" Tony demanded.

"I had to leave." Caroline defended herself hotly. "It was business."

Tony stared at her. "Come on, Caroline. You couldn't even let him drive you into town?"

"It would've taken too long," she argued.

"I don't think so." Tony shook his head. "I think you were just scared of making another mistake...like the last time you got really involved with a guy."

Caroline fidgeted in her seat. "That was ages ago."

"Ah, but the humiliation from it is still painfully fresh, am I right?"

Caroline was silent a long moment. Finally, she said, "For a brother, you sure are a pain."

"I know." Tony grinned. They exchanged glances once again. "Stop torturing yourself," he advised. "Go for him."

Caroline only wished it were that simple. "It's too late."

"It's never too late."

"He's not going to forgive me," Caroline said. In mere days, he'd gone on to make a new life for himself, trading in his Memorial Drive town house for a sumptuous home in River Oaks...not too far from her own. Obviously he'd meant what he said about settling down. And obviously, from the many women he was publicly squiring around, he was determined to find someone suitable as soon as possible.

Tony frowned at her. "I agree. He sure as hell won't forgive you if you sit here and do nothing."

"FOR A MAN WHO HAS all of his seven sisters under one roof for the first time in three years, you sure don't look very happy," Rick's sister Leslie, said.

Rick paused in the act of tying his bow tie. "It shows?"

"From the looks of things, you have everything you've ever wanted."

Except Caroline. Rick slipped on his black tuxedo jacket. With her, he had blown it, big-time.

"Wealth, social standing, any number of thriving businesses. So why so glum, brother dear?" Leslie asked.

"I'm not glum."

"Uh-huh." She closed the distance between them swiftly, straightened his bow tie and pinched his cheek in a motherly fashion. "This is your party face?"

He gave her a droll look. "I'm just worried about the—uh—caterers," he fibbed.

"Sure." Leslie crossed her arms in front of her.

Rick defended himself hotly. "Hey, it's my first big party in this house."

"Right."

"I don't want anything to go wrong."

Leslie continued to study him. "You're not over her, are you?"

"Her who?" Rick asked.

"Caroline Lord, that's who!"

Rick shrugged, as if it hardly mattered, when in reality it was the only thing that seemed to matter at all in his life these days. "We broke up weeks ago," he said.

"Yeah," Leslie agreed, "and you've been a real stick-in-the-mud ever since."

"I've dated."

"Legions," his sister agreed. "All of them beautiful. All of them bright, successful. You've had your picture in the society page any number of times. And yet," she surmised slowly, "you still look like a man who just lost his best friend."

Rick shrugged and slapped on some after-shave, the kind Caroline had liked. "I got used to being engaged, that's all," he said. "I'll get used to being free, too."

"Somehow I don't think so," Leslie observed dryly.

"Why not?"

"Because Caroline Lord was different from all the others, that's why not."

"Not so different. She was married to her career."

"So?" Leslie protested, looking scandalized. "So are you."

"Yeah, well, I never would've put the business first, especially after..."

"After what?" Leslie prompted when he didn't continued.

After the night we had. He'd never felt such passion with any woman. And he had thought, erroneously, Rick supposed, that Caroline felt that way, too. He'd thought that what they had shared was very, very special. Worth a lifetime commitment. Worth any adjustments either of them might have to make to ensure a life together. Boy, had he been wrong, Rick thought sourly. Caroline Lord didn't give an inch. Never had, never would.

"I just wouldn't have, that's all," Rick finally replied.

"Wait a minute. Am I talking to the same man who posed as a caterer to meet Caroline Lord?"

"That was business," Rick corrected.

"Oh. So it's okay for *you* to put business first. Just not her."

Rick sighed. Leslie was deliberately taking this all wrong.

"Caroline Lord has responsibilities, Rick, responsibilities unlike you've ever dreamed," Leslie continued, sounding less like his sister and more like a teacher lecturing an errant student.

"I know about responsibilities," Rick said. "Have you forgotten? I run my own businesses, too."

"Yes, but until you hooked up with Caroline, you never had all of Houston watching you do it. Waiting for you to make a mistake or fail. The family name and your father's legend in the cosmetics business, wasn't all tied up in whether you succeeded or not. She's under enormous pressure, Rick. She wants to do well. Not just for her sake, but for the sake of her father's memory. Can you really blame her for doing everything possible to protect that?"

"She still should have put us first," Rick insisted stubbornly, knowing in his heart it was true.

"Maybe she did. Maybe in her heart, you were first. Maybe she just didn't know how to show it,"

Leslie pointed out calmly. "Maybe, like everything else in life, it takes practice to learn how to let go of work and hold on to your mate."

"You're saying I should give her another chance?" Rick retorted impatiently.

Leslie merely raised a brow. "You're telling me you shouldn't?"

"WHAT DO YOU MEAN there's no food?" Rick asked. He was in the process of punching numbers into the phone. He paused and stood there numbly, receiver in hand.

"Exactly what I said," his sister Francine repeated. "The caterers are here. They brought all the glasses and dishes but they said you were to supply the food. That you had hired another firm—a local restaurant, they thought—to do the actual preparation. They say you hired them only to serve and clean up."

Rick stared at Francine, sure this must be a joke. The front doorbell was ringing. Cars were lining up in the drive. Some celebration this was turning out to be. He set the phone back down with a thud. He'd wanted to call Caroline. Why, he wasn't sure. Perhaps to apologize. His mouth thinned. "Where's the person in charge?"

"In the kitchen. Aren't you going to get the door?"

"You get the door, Francine," Rick said. "I'll straighten out this mess." Rick just hoped it could be straightened out.

He strode through the wide marble hall and into the kitchen. He blinked. What was his sister talking about? he wondered. There was plenty of food. And plenty of help. Everybody was dressed in austere gray uniforms. Except one. The lady backing into the kitchen was dressed in a ridiculously short, ridiculously tight French maid's uniform. She wore seamed black stockings and high heels. Her glorious mane of bittersweet chocolate had been swept up into an efficient-looking knot on the back of her head.

Rick's heartbeat speeded up. He knew that heart-shaped derriere. Knew it well! His pulse racing, he sauntered forward just as she nearly dropped her tray. Acting quickly, he rescued it from her delicate hands.

"Thanks." She glanced up, for a moment looked just as stunned to see him as he was to see her. Her delectable lips fell open as the color flooded her cheeks. "Rick!"

He took her hand.

"Where are we going?" she asked, albeit a little huskily.

"You'll see," Rick promised.

He led her quickly up the back stairs and into his bedroom. It was neat as a pin. Striding to the closet, he reached in and pulled out a handful of clothes and tossed them around the room. Then he dashed to the window, looked down into the drive and gasped loudly for comic effect. He dashed right back to her side. "Kiss me."

Caroline was laughing and blushing. "What?" she asked.

He thought she'd never looked so pretty as she did at that moment. "Don't ask questions," Rick demanded, sliding his arms around her back. He bent her backward, until her weight rested along his thigh. "Just..." He lowered his mouth to hers slowly, relishing every inch of anticipation. "Kiss me."

Their lips met. Heat flowed. The unhappiness he'd been feeling left him. Rick sighed and lifted his mouth from hers. "Somehow, it seems as if we've done this all before," he drawled with a roguishly provoking grin. Once, making love with her would've been enough. Now he wanted so much more.

"Except—" Caroline broke away from him. She sashayed over to his bed with a provocative sway of her hips and tossed back, then rumpled the covers on his bed.

"*Now* it's familiar." She plopped down on the sheets.

His spirits soaring, he sat down beside her and took her hand in his. He wasn't sure what her showing up here like this meant. He only knew it was a good sign.

"We didn't do this." He slid a hand behind her and drew her gently down, so they were lying across the bed, with Caroline cozily ensconced in his arms. Maybe if he were persuasive enough, she'd want more, too.

She laced her arms around his neck. "Not that night," Caroline agreed. She touched her index finger to his lips. "But I wanted to," she whispered.

"So did I."

A heartbeat passed, then another. Rick couldn't seem to stop staring at her. "I've missed you," he said huskily.

Caroline's hazel eyes gleamed moistly. "I've missed you, too," she said unsteadily.

Rick's heart was pounding. There was a roaring in his ears and an answering tension in his thighs. "Does this mean—?" Not wanting to take too much for granted, he left the thought hanging.

Caroline nodded earnestly. She clasped him tightly. Her eyes never left his face. "I want us to try again, Rick. For real this time," she said in a strong, clear voice.

Rick swallowed. "It was real the last time," he countered softly.

"I know, but it wasn't supposed to be that way."

"True."

They stared at one another, marveling at the sheer wonder of their togetherness. "And there's something else," Caroline said, her eyes going all soft and misty again.

He was busy taking the pins from her hair and getting rid of her ridiculous white lace hat. "What?"

Caroline drew a deep breath. "I was wrong to leave you the way I did at the beach house," she admitted. "I know that now. I should have waited for you."

Rick sighed and rolled onto his back. He stared up at the ceiling, wishing she hadn't brought up that unhappy time. "Why didn't you?" he asked, recalling how hurt and stunned and angry he had been.

Caroline rolled over, too, and rested both arms and her chin on his chest. She looked into his eyes and spoke the words straight from her heart. "Because I was afraid."

"Afraid?" Unable to help himself, he sifted a hand through the dark silk of her hair.

"Afraid you didn't love me the way I love you. And I do love you, Rick," she said softly, "with all my heart."

"I love you, too." Rick gripped her arms and pulled her up, so their mouths were at equal level. He kissed her lightly.

"What happened was my fault, too," he said. His eyes darkened possessively. "I should have been more understanding. Maxwell Lord isn't just a business to you. It's part of the Lord family. A part of Max, and Tony and you. It's something you want to give your children, and hope they'll give theirs."

Caroline grinned and relief sparkled in her eyes. "You do understand."

"Yes." Rick nodded. "I know that you love Maxwell Lord as much as you loved your father, that you grew up here and that the traditions of the company are ones you want to uphold. I want you to do that, too."

They cuddled together, content. Caroline ran a hand over the hardness of his chest. She loved the way he felt. She loved his strength. "I'll always have time for you, Rick."

"I know."

A tremulous sigh escaped her lips. "I can't promise there won't be crises."

He rolled so she was beneath him once again. "There will."

"But we'll handle them together next time," she promised tenderly, as her gaze roved his face. "I won't shut you out."

"Then that leaves only one thing left to settle," Rick said, loving the way she felt beneath him, so soft and feminine and strong.

Caroline stopped in the act of running her index fingers along his lower lip and looked puzzled. "What?"

"The wedding," Rick said, his mouth still tingling lightly from her experimental caress. He lifted her hand to his mouth and sucked on her fingers lightly. "When is it going to take place?" He asked as a familiar, faintly luminous look came into her eyes.

Caroline groaned. "Mother just started a new miniseries. She'll want to be here."

"We certainly can't have a wedding without her," Rick agreed. After all, Marjorie had gotten the two of them together in the first place.

Caroline bit her lip indecisively. She smoothed her hands through his hair, pushing it away from his ears, then reached around the back of his neck to cup his head. She looked very much like she was considering kissing him, the conversation, their plans, the guests downstairs, all be damned. "Do you think we can wait two months?" She sighed languidly, the impatient shifting of her body beneath him letting him know she didn't want to wait even two more minutes for them to be together again.

Rick bent his head to hers. "For the wedding, sure," he said as he began to kiss her in all the old, familiar, wonderful ways. "But the loving starts right now."

OFFICIAL RULES • MILLION DOLLAR MATCH 3 SWEEPSTAKES
NO PURCHASE OR OBLIGATION NECESSARY TO ENTER

To enter, follow the directions published. **ALTERNATE MEANS OF ENTRY:** Hand print your name and address on a 3" × 5" card and mail to either: Harlequin "Match 3," 3010 Walden Ave., P.O. Box 1867, Buffalo, NY 14269-1867 or Harlequin "Match 3," P.O. Box 609, Fort Erie, Ontario L2A 5X3, and we will assign your Sweepstakes numbers. (Limit: one entry per envelope.) For eligibility, entries must be received no later than March 31, 1994. No responsibility is assumed for lost, late or misdirected entries.

Upon receipt of entry, Sweepstakes numbers will be assigned. To determine winners, Sweepstakes numbers will be compared against a list of randomly preselected prizewinning numbers. In the event all prizes are not claimed via the return of prizewinning numbers, random drawings will be held from among all other entries received to award unclaimed prizes.

Prizewinners will be determined no later than May 30, 1994. Selection of winning numbers and random drawings are under the supervision of D.L. Blair, Inc., an independent judging organization, whose decisions are final. One prize to a family or organization. No substitution will be made for any prize, except as offered. Taxes and duties on all prizes are the sole responsibility of winners. Winners will be notified by mail. Chances of winning are determined by the number of entries distributed and received.

Sweepstakes open to persons 18 years of age or older, except employees and immediate family members of Torstar Corporation, D.L. Blair, Inc., their affiliates, subsidiaries and all other agencies, entities and persons connected with the use, marketing or conduct of this Sweepstakes. All applicable laws and regulations apply. Sweepstakes offer void wherever prohibited by law. Any litigation within the province of Quebec respecting the conduct and awarding of a prize in this Sweepstakes must be submitted to the Régies des Loteries et Courses du Quebec. In order to win a prize, residents of Canada will be required to correctly answer a time-limited arithmetical skill-testing question. Values of all prizes are in U.S. currency.

Winners of major prizes will be obligated to sign and return an affidavit of eligibility and release of liability within 30 days of notification. In the event of non-compliance within this time period, prize may be awarded to an alternate winner. Any prize or prize notification returned as undeliverable will result in the awarding of that prize to an alternate winner. By acceptance of their prize, winners consent to use of their names, photographs or other likenesses for purposes of advertising, trade and promotion on behalf of Torstar Corporation without further compensation, unless prohibited by law.

This Sweepstakes is presented by Torstar Corporation, its subsidiaries and affiliates in conjunction with book, merchandise and/or product offerings. Prizes are as follows: Grand Prize—$1,000,000 (payable at $33,333.33 a year for 30 years). First through Sixth Prizes may be presented in different creative executions, each with the following approximate values: First Prize—$35,000; Second Prize—$10,000; 2 Third Prizes—$5,000 each; 5 Fourth Prizes—$1,000 each; 10 Fifth Prizes—$250 each; 1,000 Sixth Prizes—$100 each. Prizewinners will have the opportunity of selecting any prize offered for that level. A travel-prize option, if offered and selected by winner, must be completed within 12 months of selection and is subject to hotel and flight accommodations availability. Torstar Corporation may present this Sweepstakes utilizing names other than Million Dollar Sweepstakes. For a current list of all prize options offered within prize levels and all names the Sweepstakes may utilize, send a self-addressed, stamped envelope (WA residents need not affix return postage) to: Million Dollar Sweepstakes Prize Options/Names, P.O. Box 4710, Blair, NE 68009.

The Extra Bonus Prize will be awarded in a random drawing to be conducted no later than May 30, 1994 from among all entries received. To qualify, entries must be received by March 31, 1994 and comply with published directions. No purchase necessary. For complete rules, send a self-addressed, stamped envelope (WA residents need not affix return postage) to: Extra Bonus Prize Rules, P.O. Box 4600, Blair, NE 68009.

For a list of prizewinners (available after July 31, 1994) send a separate, stamped, self-addressed envelope to: Million Dollar Sweepstakes Winners, P.O. Box 4728, Blair, NE 68009.

SWP-H693

THREE UNFORGETTABLE HEROINES
THREE AWARD-WINNING AUTHORS

MAVERICK HEARTS

A unique collection of historical short stories that capture the spirit of America's last frontier.

HEATHER GRAHAM POZZESSERE—over 10 million copies of her books in print worldwide
Lonesome Rider—The story of an Eastern widow and the renegade half-breed who becomes her protector.

PATRICIA POTTER—an author whose books are consistently Waldenbooks bestsellers
Against the Wind—Two people, battered by heartache, prove that love can heal all.

JOAN JOHNSTON—award-winning Western historical author with 17 books to her credit
One Simple Wish—A woman with a past discovers that dreams really do come true.

Join us for an exciting journey West with
UNTAMED
Available in July, wherever Harlequin books are sold.

MAV93

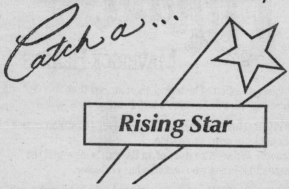